chameleon

(days)

chameleon (days)

A Novel

Dean Serravalle

| N₁ | O₂ | N₁

CANADA

Library and Archives Canada Cataloguing in Publication

Serravalle, Dean, 1973–, author
Chameleon (days) / Dean Serravalle.

ISBN 978–1–988098–48–7 (softcover)

I. Title.

PS8587.E7748C43 2018   C813'.6   C2018–900450–9

Printed and bound in Canada on 100% recycled paper.

Now Or Never Publishing
901, 163 Street
Surrey, British Columbia
Canada V4A 9T8

nonpublishing.com
Fighting Words.

We gratefully acknowledge the support of the Canada Council for the Arts
and the British Columbia Arts Council for our publishing program.

For Tommy (Roselli)

DAY I

AUTHOR'S (IN YOUR) PREFACE

I've killed the man in me who pleases. The one who cares about doing the right thing the right way. The man who works for an invisible audience. Whoever you are, whatever you are, wherever you are—I don't suffer for you anymore. What you may expect from the way I tell this story. Especially since I am trespassing inside of it already.

I had a writing instructor once who called this particular sin "authorial intrusion." She said an author shouldn't interfere with the story he is creating. Arrest me, then. For this is exactly what I am about to do. Intrude. Break into the story. Rob it. Leave some shit behind, maybe a trademark or two. It's going to feel like you lost something at the end. This poetic mess you won't want to clean up.

And I may rob the story more than once, to be honest. Come back and find new items in it to steal. I may be so mean as to take your photo albums on the way out. This is my wife's greatest fear if the house should ever burn down. Hey, there's an idea. Set the story on fire at one point. Maybe after I rob it, but before it resolves itself? Why not? No one is paying me to write you a fancy story. If anything, I may have to kill myself first for someone to publish it.

Or, you can just put the book back on the shelf. Again, why not? Why should you listen to this wash-up, or read the story he stole from a naked girl who fell asleep on his soft pillow and let it drool from her mouth. She doesn't even know I stole it, by the way. Too bad. The characters are mine now, the fiction is mine, her truth is mine, the untruth is mine, and its virginity is mine, except, I am not going to parade this story down an isle with a white dress. . . .

No, no, no, this story is broken, into, officially, and it starts with a guy I met in my walk-in closet. Actually, he wasn't really there but I hear him speaking to me whenever I change in the dark. You see, I don't want to wake my wife. She knows I have to go to work and the kids need to sleep in the quiet morning night. Ever try finding a shirt to match your pants in the dark? How about a tie to bring out the dominant colour of your patterned socks? It is always cold in the closet too. Whoever built the house must have thought clothes don't need warmth. The hardwood floor is a sheet of ice. The room is dark and my wife's silky dresses lick my back as I smell what's fresh on my side, what's dry-cleaner chemical on my skin, the dull scent of a brown, neck-stained collar.

In this same closet, a fictional character introduces himself to me whenever he believes no one else is listening. He is the fictional character who appears first in this story. A skinny vegan type of man with skull bones pocking the skin on his face. White hair traces a receding "M" on his forehead. To be frank, I met him in the shower first. He's kind of obsessed with me when I have privacy. In the shower. On the toilet. In the car on my way to London. In the dark, cold, walk-in closet, or when I grab some hung sausage from the cellar downstairs. He follows me around like a kid believing you have candy in your pocket, even though you ate it right in front of him.

Like I said, he's the guy who appears first in my stolen story. This man who wears a three piece suit wherever he goes because he needs an inside pocket to hang a watch on. He likes the feel of it ticking against his belly. It reminds him of fleeting time. It reminds him of the value of life because he has taken so many.

He waits in a grotto for a hired messenger. The grotto is one I visited myself on Mount Gargano. As a teenager, I took great interest in this underground cavern. Water drips down its carved out walls and a mysterious stream flows behind them. A local saint is buried in a glass coffin so that tourists could see she never decomposed, while a statue of Saint Michael the Archangel is tucked into a little cove. He overlooks a drift of candles below him. In his famous pose, his sword is about to attack their evaporating light. I was told by a pilgrimage priest if I wished for anything in the grotto; it would be granted to me. A local, folklore secret, so it didn't surprise me to see crutches decorating the cavern wall. Pictures taped to it. Scratched in thank you messages. I made a wish myself, but not for this character, who never deals with uncertainty.

His name has changed so many times it is a question mark to his own memory. So I will call him "The Man". Simple enough. The Man waits in the grotto for The Messenger. The Messenger he will see alive for the last time. The Messenger he has learned about through every investigative means necessary. His knowledge of The Messenger is godlike privy from the inside out. His knowledge of The Messenger overflows enough to make him believe he has every right to pronounce his death. Ownership of another man does have its privileges. It justifies murder. It justifies mercy. The Man waits in the flickering dark pockets pooled by the candles, then by the glass coffin, before settling at the top of the stairway. The first step down is steep and almost invisible to the feet.

The Man will wait for The Messenger to enter the grotto. No cellular reception here. No pictures allowed. And then The Man will sneak up on The Messenger and speak to him from behind. If The Messenger manages to look back at The Man's Sodom and Gomorrah face, The Man will be forced to paralyze him permanently with a needle. He will then seek someone else to perform his mission. The Messenger knows the instruction and this consequence worse than death. He knows nothing of The Man, however, who came to life for me first, years after I stole the story—the one who talks to me from the closet, and in the shower, and sometimes in the silence after I've made love to my wife, this man with a message.

For the message is more important than The Messenger. The Man knows it. So does The Messenger. This Man from my closet does not exist to anyone but his own understanding of how the world works. He has graduated from spy conspiracies. He has graduated from the command of others. He has graduated from a fake obituary with a fake name. He exists solely in the purgatory he has devised for himself. A place built on getting away with murder. Or worse transgressions. His pocket watch ticks to remind him he is real. He is never identified. Not even as a stranger. He procures no rewards for his plotting. He serves no master or higher order. He is already presumed dead. The Messenger is only familiar with what The Man knows of him.

To The Messenger, The Man must be a ghost or a man in the likeness of evil. How else could The Man know him so intimately? This Man with a message.

The damp grotto is nearly empty these late evenings for those praying with half open arms. They supplicate on blistered knees by the orchestra of candles. The Man from my walk-in closet waits by the entrance until The Messenger arrives. He does so on time. He was told to arrive on the exact minute. No sooner or later. The Messenger descends to a pew where the corner candles are too damp to reignite. The Man in the three piece suit follows him there. The Messenger knows he is being followed.

The Messenger is a man in his early forties weathered elderly by the tragedies of his own life. The death of a soul mate. The death of an only child shortly thereafter. The acknowledgment of perfect health despite his own attempts at killing himself. My Man from the closet knows it all. Such criteria limited his search, refining it to a point of certainty. The Messenger wants to die more than anyone The Man has ever researched. The Messenger simply has the bad luck of being saved. Twenty-three suicide attempts and some very creative ones. Only to be saved every time. A passerby at the bottom of the cliff. A scuba diver in the canal. Helicopters before the brink of The Falls. A surgeon who expertly removed the misfired bullet from his skull.

This is no ordinary Messenger, according to my Man. This Messenger is immortal. So who better to deliver a dangerous message than one who requests death as payment?

By the way, do you see why The Man's voice scares me in the walk-in closet? My Man is a haunting figure. He leans over the rotting wood of the pew and speaks over the shoulder of The Messenger in the same, reassuring voice.

"It's okay now. You will reach your end."

The Messenger is overjoyed although he doesn't want to show it. He listens and forces himself not to look behind him.

"You will deliver a mission in a message for me."

The Messenger nods. He can feel breath on his neck and surprisingly, it is dry and warm, with no scent.

"You will travel to a village in Northern Lebanon. It is called Bsharri. The birthplace of the poet. You will access it via the Syrian border. You will find a black priest in a church there. He will lead you to a Muslim man who lives amongst his enemies. He enters Maronite churches. He makes the sign of the cross when he wishes to avoid the suspicion of his paranoid villagers. His face is clean of hair, like a newborn baby's. Twenty-three facial surgeries to absolve his true identity. All voluntary. He has one name. Kashif. It means revealing spirit. Ironically, he doesn't have one, a spirit. He has more blood on his hands than many wars. He believes himself retired from the dangerous game. His only weakness is thirteen years old. She lives in the same village without knowledge of him, in a hospital. We have a rifle pointed at her neck. Make sure you remind him of this reality."

"What is the mission?"

The Messenger regrets speaking out loud. It indicates impatience. He lowers his head.

"The mission is to rescue a child not like his own . . ."

"You will explain these details to him. This child in need of rescue is a miracle stolen and detained by the wrong faith. He is five years old and is just learning how to walk. And yet, he can cure the devil of an illness."

The Messenger tries to imagine the child.

"The child is the next coming captured. Only Kashif can deliver him. Only Kashif can infiltrate the walls he has built himself in another lifetime."

"How will he find this child?" The Messenger asks, once again hesitating to sound rude.

"With his specialty—terror. He will know how to find him. Before he decides on the mission, he will know better to shoot you in the head on the edge of a mountain cliff. You will see the width of a blue sky and white mountain peaks before everything turns to black. He will not miss. He will not let you live after you deliver this message. He will never trust the messenger or the mission, but one, you, will be available to kill, the other will pursue his greatest fear."

The Messenger understands the message. He questions one detail further.

"His daughter is already dying?"

"Yes. We will kill him before she says goodbye."

The Man delivering the message adjusts the lower button on his suit jacket. The Man rises from the pew and disappears into the crowd as he ascends the stairs to a lighter darkness. The Messenger lights a candle and offers thanks for The Man's promise.

DAY 2

The Man sits in the front seat of my truck. He tries to convince me I need to research that little village in Lebanon some more. He says I must breathe in the cedar-wooded air before I set the next scene. With my mind's voice, I tell him I don't feel like doing anything. My wife found a lump in her breast the night before. She woke me from my sleep to have me find it myself. I felt it below the softness of her skin—lurking.

The Man from the preface will not appear anywhere in the next chapter of this story. However, his temporary exit from the story doesn't mean he doesn't care for it. I can hear him in my inner ear as I drive to work. It is early in the morning and I follow the leftover moon in the sky alongside the highway.

"You need to do me justice," The Man repeats.

I assume justice means I have to write a story worthy of his participation in it. I'm sure he's read The Preface already, since he inspired it. And it wouldn't surprise me if he didn't approve, although he hasn't mentioned anything specific about it yet. I'm sure he likes that I've rewritten it a few times already. For an outcast, private character, he seems to seek public attention or at least all of mine.

I wait in a traffic line to enter the school parking lot. Parents who refuse their children the horror of riding a yellow bus to school clog the entranceway. They try to swing in ahead of the busses. And then they try to pass them on the left when all of the cars are stationary. I want to listen to music but I can't. I don't want to appear rude to The Man. I feel a duty to our telepathic conversation now that I have written him on a page. And I am distracted. I have four children. I don't want them to grow up without a mother.

When I finally reach my class, Mr. Lye, one of the vice principals, is waiting at my door. He is a stout man with a grey spotted goatee moustache. He is upset with me.

"You need to be in class," he points to my door's entrance. The bell hasn't rung yet.

I don't say anything, although the few students sitting at their desks send him daggers with their eyes. They protect me by spiting him more. He picks at their uniforms, confronts them when they are flirting with each other in the hallways and stops music at dances to reprimand their sexual gyrations. In return, they make him the enemy for his job description.

My first period kids are locally developed, which means they are reading at levels much lower than their ages. I feel for The Man from my Preface when I reach the classroom, knowing they take higher priority. Luckily for the both of us, he has disappeared for a while.

"You have another grey hair, sir," Emily points out. I have many on my head now, which leads me to believe she solely wants to start a conversation that will transition into one of her weekend trailer stories. She lives in a foster trailer home, but she sells the experience frequently as an amusement park.

The Man finally takes a seat in the class and I can see him nodding his head at me. Although he harasses me more in private, he realizes my creative spirit needs a room to be alone in. He suggests calling the other vice principal. He wants me to fictionalize a story of illness, so I can go home and continue research on this tiny village in Lebanon, where The Messenger is headed. To kill two birds with one enormous shotgun, I do him one better. I venture into the hallway to find one of our Lebanese exchange students. His name is Mohammed and he is Muslim. He loves soccer and he knows I played, so he is always trash talking me on lunch duty. I find him at his locker.

"Hey Mohammed, I need some information on a tiny village in Lebanon."

"You plan on visiting Lebanon, sir?"

"No, just writing about it."

"Can I be in the story?"

"Yeah, yeah, yeah. Listen. It's called Bsharri. It's a Catholic village in the north."

"I'm from Beirut, sir."

"I know that, Mohammed."

"Okay, let me text my father and I will get back to you."

"Thanks," I say, while Mr. Lye roams the hallways to clear them before morning prayer announcements. The bell still hasn't rung. I worry if seeking research about a tiny village in Lebanon is appropriate behaviour for a husband who felt a lump in his wife's breast this morning.

The Man, my character from the Preface, is happy I took the initiative. As the author of the story, I feel like I shouldn't have to answer to a character, never mind one who isn't my protagonist. Yet, he is insistent like the coach who was never the best player. It's a priority that the story he is a part of comes alive with my fiction, despite its root of truth.

I'm not his slave, I say under my breath. Emily stares at me. She is always staring at me in the front row, with her magnifying eyes, trying to find one more grey hair or a longer one sliding out of a nostril, or a fluff of some on my ears. Maybe she is my ticking clock, personified. Maybe she is the pocket watch that reminds me I have to get this story down on paper, when in actuality, life needs to happen first.

My kids need to eat. I need to sleep. My kids need light. I need to pay electricity bills. My wife needs to see a doctor only my benefits can pay for. Where does writing a story fit into these more pressing realities?

"It fills in the spaces worth dreaming about in between them, stupid," I hear my Man saying. I can imagine him smirking somewhere, although I know he hates my digressions.

On my lunch duty, Mohammed finds me. He is eating a pita wrap and I can see creamy hummus on his tongue as he talks at the same time.

"This village you asked me about. It surrounds a church. Actually, the homes are so close to the church you can hear the confessions from within it," he laughs more at the Catholic ritual of confessing your sins. I can tell his father finds the practice weak in this young boy's Muslim voice. Although, not weak enough to send his son to a Catholic school.

"Why are they so close?" I ask.

"The church protects them from the inside. The cedar trees and the mountains protect the village from the outside."

"From what?"

"From storms, earthquakes, us."

Mohammed laughs again. His skin is dark, oily and pimple ridden, like the rest of the kids. Unlike them, his attitude is very condescending. Even to his fourth period English teacher from last year.

"The village protects itself against conversion?" I ask.

He nods.

"Are you planning on moving there, sir?"

His jokes are as garlicy as his breath.

"No, I'm deporting you there, Mohammed."

"You won't find me dead there, sir."

His roots show.

"Isn't that the point?" I joke and he finds it funny until another bite.

I call my wife after lunch duty but she doesn't respond. She is supposed to contact her doctor and arrange a mammogram. I shirk at the horrible possibilities of what such a test may find. And I think of my cousin who passed the year before. My age, and much more brilliant with his hands. But also, four kids.

After school, I get on my phone and research this tiny village. Bsharri. The pictures preach escapism. Apparently it roots the only remaining Original Cedars of Lebanon. Tall, multi-trunked cedar trees whose exposed roots cling to mountain cliffs like arms climbing them. The peak of the church attempts to rise from the valley and is gratefully shielded by the green. Historically, Bsharri in Phoenician translation means 'The House of Ishtar,' which alludes to the worship of a pagan goddess. And yet, Maronite Christians sought refuge in the mountainous terrain when they were persecuted in the 7TH Century. Characterized by its courageous and tribal resistance, the people of Bsharri are very hospitable but violently patriotic, which may explain why Kashif, the man who will receive the message, hides there. He hides in a land renowned for its resistance against Palestinian and Syrian invasions. A beautiful northern landscape of mountains and valleys, with a church nestled expertly in the valley.

The Messenger has these pictures on his phone as well. He glances at them periodically to imagine Kashif, the man unaware of the message he is about to receive. The Messenger is more invested in his dying scene, or, rather, where he imagines himself to be murdered. It excites him. The thought of finally dying and not by his own failed hand. He considers it justified now. His intentions have always dictated this fate with mind body spirit communication breakdowns preventing the proper execution of this desire. The Messenger trusts my Man. He trusts the voice that reassured him he would die on the mountain, his last vision of the sky in the pictures.

The Messenger reverts to these pictures the hotter it gets on the bus he is travelling on. He is in Syria and the roads are pothole ridden and sink hole cavernous at times. The bus rocks to the point of keeling over. Instinctively, passengers leap from their seats to the other side to balance it. It is plain and evident that assembled families are fleeing with the hope of gaining access to the border, although The Messenger can read other designs in their dust dried eyes. Making a run for it in the opposite direction, for instance.

The Messenger must find a way to cross the border. He has no passport. If he did, it would only serve to stall his entrance. Or prevent him entirely with a detention. He must smuggle his way across the border and he carries enough bribe money in his pocket to do so. He is also not afraid to kill anyone in his way since he is not afraid to die by retaliation. But he is also a man of promise. One who values a vow. He never sought another woman after his wife died. He never considered moving on to another life. And when his own child died, he felt no inclination to start anew. Instead, every second thought about them hollowed him further, like a butcher carving meat from his bones without the need to skin him first. His bones rattle when their images race through his hollow, cavernous tunnels, leaving only empty echoes in the darkness of forgetting.

He walks up to the bus driver and asks him to open the door. It is practically parked in a line of beeping lorries. The Messenger would prefer to walk across the border on foot. Once on the other side, he could always hitchhike his way to the village of Bsharri or find another bus. Crossing the line is the challenge. Green Beret-clad men with shouldered machine artillery pace lines and point the tips of guns into windows to incite facial recognition. A few of them catch him walking towards them with his hands up. As he does so, he finds interested eyes in the eldest of the group, the leader. The Messenger adjusts the direction of his path to meet with this general.

"What do you think you are doing?" the official asks. His accent is silky Persian.

"Crossing the border."

The Messenger is fluent in sixty-four languages. He once worked as a translator for the United Nations before his promotion to diplomatic peace missions. He learned negotiation skills and the art of reading a lying face in this capacity. He found the right man to bribe at the border. He communicates this mutual understanding by lowering his hands and becoming a close talker. Not necessarily a pleasurable tactic, it communicates trust and secrecy to the official with body language. The official with a beret seemingly stapled to his head by metal pins and symbols is equally as tall. His stomach protrudes to the brink of his shirt buttons, while his gun holster disappears below the rounded belly. He is a man of appetite, The Messenger deduces.

He points his gun into The Messenger's chest to protect his space. It indents The Messenger's chest like the point of a knife.

"Turn around."

The Messenger does as he is told. The point of the gun finds the imaginary passage of the bullet on The Messenger's back, if he would have pulled the trigger.

"Walk."

All of the subservient officials glance over to the scene briefly. They are too afraid to stare. The Messenger finds himself in a closet inside the customs building. In the dark again. He hates the dark for making his memories come to life like a projector film. The Messenger squints his eyes hard in an attempt to create white stars and flashes, maybe even a headache. These are physical distractions he has devised, psychological horse shutters.

He can't prevent the smell of cleanliness, bleach from the mop bucket, to spur on a back door entrance to a memory.

His baby son is floating in the kitchen sink. Tiny, small enough to fit in, like a dish or a fragile glass. His wife is pulling her hair back and he sees her freckled neck in this memory. It is youthful and the skin is taut on her throat. She is laughing and his son is splashing. There is water on the ceramic tile of the floor. He had just returned from a trip in Egypt to make the birth a few days prior. Although his baby is blind and his eyes haven't come into focus, his first born is gripping his arm instinctively as if holding onto a safety bar. He is insecure in his own bath water, in the warmth of his mother's singing, so he has reached out for a lifeline. The Messenger never wants to leave his home again. There is too much to lose now.

The official arrives having changed out of his uniform. He looks like a father himself in civilian khaki slacks and a Hawaiian patterned shirt.

"Come with me."

The Messenger follows the official who appears to have finished his shift. The official leads him to a dressing room. He walks in to make sure the institutional shower area is vacated. He then proceeds to pull a uniform from a locker.

"Change."

The Messenger does as he is told, removing the envelope of money from his pocket to remind the official of his payment.

The thickness of the envelope indicates more danger, which makes the official too honest to steal it outright. He seems to understand there are other powers at work greater than his sphere of influence. He waits until The Messenger has fully dressed.

"You, my soldier, will drive me home."

The official throws The Messenger the keys.

"I always have a soldier drive me home."

The Messenger is curious to know why, yet he doesn't ask. The official explains anyway.

"To protect the money I take."

This confession confuses The Messenger.

"To each his share."

The Messenger feels like he has met a man whose name should be The Collector. A man with an understanding of a role. A man devoted to one destiny, like his own.

"I will leave you on the side of the road somewhere."

Of course, thinks The Messenger. He didn't expect a ride anywhere to begin with. This needs to be a pilgrimage, at the end of which exists the story of a tragedy or a visitation. When he starts the car his heart beats at the possibility of a car bomb about to detonate. And for some reason, he is disappointed when he sees the fuel gauge at full and ready to roll.

I decide not to conclude this chapter because I hear my wife entering upstairs. The kids are asleep and the baby monitor downstairs sounds like one long raspy breath. When I hear the heaviness of the steel door seal the fumes of the minivan inside the garage, I join her at the island in the kitchen. She is already drinking a glass of water. I don't ask her how the appointment went because I can see the signed requisition for a test sticking to the countertop. She stares at me through the clear glass as she drinks. I can tell she is worried. I can hear it in her hard swallows, how thirsty she is.

"Are you ready to go to bed?" I ask.

She nods and I follow her up the stairs.

Day 3

It doesn't take long for the border official to discard The Messenger. As soon as they cross the border into the village of Kaa in the Bekaa Valley, he removes a gun hidden under his belly and places it flat on his knee.

"Stop the car here."

The Messenger sees poverty outside in the mountain refracted sunset. A collection of homes, mosques, churches, and damaged settlements scatter themselves on a rock embedded plain. Treed thicket areas are strafed into thinned out withering sticks. This place is polluted by its own history.

The official extends his other hand to shake good-bye.

"Thank you."

The Messenger didn't expect the entire exchange to be so polite, so absent of conflict. He supposes the bribe made his illegal crossing friendly to the man. In an obvious attempt to give The Messenger more for his money, the official assumes a tour guide's voice.

"This is Kaa. You will find everything you need here. Catholics, Shiites, Melkites, hard faced extremists. Ask the right questions to the wrong people and they will help."

Upon opening the car door, The Messenger breathes in sulphur instead of air. He closes the door and asks one more question through an open window.

"Bsharri?"

"You are close. This is the ground of martyrs. Respect the soil."

The Messenger finds it difficult to understand the official's code language. It resembles a dialect mutated from a foreign time.

The official drives off into the dust and disappears into another winding valley. Sensing the coolness of night, The

Messenger walks into a town-like collection of stone buildings. He sees dark men smoking outside. They regard him with little interest. He considers venturing into a place of worship, changes his direction and settles instead for a tiny Inn. On his way there, he witnesses a heated exchange between two men. One man, the shorter one, ends the conversation by shooting the other. After he does so, he waves his family in from a parked car. A woman fully veiled rushes a blanketed newborn into the building. Two other boys remove shovels from the trunk. They deliver one to their father. The two boys dig into the rocky ground and the scrape of the shovel scratches the sky's silence. The surviving man stares at The Messenger long enough to convince him he didn't see a thing. The woman turns on the light and The Messenger can already smell olive oil burning from a pan.

At the Inn, The Messenger pays the lady wearing a niqab for a room. The Messenger makes his way there with a decoratively rusted key on a ring. A knock on the door sounds a minute later. He assumes it is someone with towels or clean sheets, both absent in the room. It is the man who shot the other. He holds a bottle without a label in his hands. Two plastic glasses rest in between his fingers and above his knuckles.

He raises them first for fear The Messenger speaks another language. The Messenger nods yes and reveals he speaks Arabic. The man smiles warmly. He wears a thin moustache, as if pinned to his face, and his black hair is youthful on his wrinkly forehead.

"It is strong."

The Messenger nods to go on and pour.

"Bsharri?"

"You are close."

The man toasts him.

"May Allah be with you."

The Messenger nods again.

"There is no police in Kaa."

The Messenger hadn't asked, but the murdering man must have felt the need to explain his crime.

"Kaa is the woman we rape when we need to. I am a lucky man. I have a new home now."

He toasts again. The Messenger reciprocates the same. The liquor tastes of black licorice.

"We are better than the Syrians, that is for sure. I would have killed you too if you resembled one."

"It took us almost thirty years to push them away. And then they came back a few years ago. They flooded the fields and then burned them down. We killed too many, almost all of them. Some days we still think they are here, rising from their graves in the rock ground."

He gets up and walks over to the window. He points to little white sheds in the distance.

"That is Ersal, a Sunni village. We call it the 'Kaa projects.' It made the Christians fly away."

He forces a laugh which ends in a violent cough. When he stops talking, The Messenger can hear the scrape of shovels conversing into the night.

"Now it is all Al-Nusra and Hezbollah. They keep order. If only they can stop the rocket bombs from the other side."

This detail explains the sporadic presence of life in Kaa. One house alone, as if in the middle of a road. Two others launched from their foundation to another area. So many rocks above ground. Granite boulders. The omniscient scent of burning flesh permeates the air like an ongoing holocaust.

"Exile is a beautiful word in Kaa," the man continues to narrate into his glass.

The man returns to his seat and they listen to the music of the shovels.

"At least I did him the courtesy of a burial," are his last words. The Messenger automatically understands how lucky he was to find a man with a heart in Kaa.

The next morning this murdering man offers the murdered man's car for The Messenger to reach Bsharri. It won't take long to reach his destination, he assures The Messenger. The Messenger receives the favour gratefully, although the man treats it as payment for forgetting what he witnessed the night before.

The young boys digging the grave had cleaned the vehicle for him. The Messenger appreciates their obedience to their father's wishes.

DAY 4

My wife finds me surrounded by papers. She creeps up on me late in the night. It's the only time I reserve the quiet to write. Otherwise, I am sharper in the morning. She doesn't say a word to me. She side steps the papers on the floor like mines and curls up on the loveseat in my office, below our framed university degrees. The glow on the walls is softened blue from the computer screen.

"What are you researching?"

She breaks the circle of paper open by pulling an article onto her lap.

"A village in Lebanon."

"Where your former wife lived?"

"My former wife never lived in Lebanon."

I can tell she isn't interested in the story. I sense instead she may be sparring for a war. After the rejection of my last two literary novels, she finally spoke her mind. She practically commanded me to write 'easier' stories to read. She likes thrillers, series led by feminist detectives, or those marked for every letter in the alphabet. A for About to Murder, B for Before Murder. You know, the stuff that sells. The books with colourful covers and wealthier authors in professional shots on the back. She supports me but not really. The recent pressure of upcoming physical tests may have made her point more difficult to suppress politely, that point being 'make some fucking money with these books.'

"Your former wife is Lebanese."

"Yes. You know she is."

She rolls her eyes and pretends to sift through the article.

"Why don't you write something about your family, at least?"

The 'at least' is the hint, of course. If you won't write what will surely make us money, then 'at least' write about something you know, like the back of your hand, or the colour of your eyes.

She is wearing her glasses, which means she couldn't sleep either. She doesn't like when I leave the warmth of the bed to find a cold leather seat in the office. She curls herself up some more, her knees at her chin.

"So why are you writing about your ex-wife again?"

She prods. I giggle it away.

"This isn't her story."

"Whose is it then?"

"Someone else's."

"So you stole this story?"

"Kind of. It was offered up to me, willingly, but I took it without her knowing."

"Her?"

I slipped. This could be the trigger point for the argument we haven't had yet since discovering the lump in her breast. The girl I've never spoken about to anyone.

"Just someone I helped a while back."

"Before you knew me?"

"Before I knew you were alive."

Not the greatest choice of words. That's for sure. She seems disgusted with me. In her eyes, I can read judgment for leaving her alone to think. Her mannerisms beg for a magic trick, like the queen expecting distraction from a hired fool. What am I paying you for, then, her body language seems to speak. We're married, not divorced like you are with your other wife. Why have you escaped back into that world? Are you planning on returning to her when I am gone? Do you still love her? Do you love the son you had with her over the three children you've had with me?

Thankfully, an image from my research strikes her.

"Does this man kill the other for his house? Is that the only reason?"

"Yeah. It's a border town, just like ours. Except it is war ravaged and invaded on a daily basis. One of my characters passes through it on his way to Bsharri."

"Bsharri?"

"Yes, it's the town where my main character resides, in secret. A village in the clouds."

"A village in the clouds, nice."

She's finally on board.

"Let me guess, it's in Lebanon too."

She just jumped off again.

"Good guess."

I could have easily defended the choice by raising my voice, but I have learned through two marriages that picking battles at two in the morning very rarely leads to makeup sex, especially when one of you believes herself to be dying already.

"Can I help?"

She surprises me with the softness of her voice in this offer. Deep down, I know she knows I need to write, despite what little income it procures for our children's futures. It seems everything we do now is directed at this target. Where they will go to school in twenty years. Who they will marry in twenty years. How can we help them for twenty years.

"Am I wasting my time?" I ask her.

"Not if you are in love with it," she says with some vinegar on the tip of her tongue.

She doesn't ask what the story or chapter is about. She doesn't ask about the characters or where they are headed in twenty years. She doesn't even skirt around the papers mapped on the hardwood floor on her way out. She steps on them, as if on purpose, and disturbs the perfect circle from which the previous chapter emerged.

When I hear her footsteps on the stairs, I run our conversation through my mind to see if I missed the hint where I inadvertently admit I don't love her the same. It seems every argument we have ever had revolves around this insecurity. If anything, I have never loved her more. Life happens in between fantasy, unfortunately, and it takes its own time to absorb into your bones.

"She doesn't understand, it's not that simple," the Man from my Preface interrupts. He takes the seat vacated by my wife in my office. He must have descended from somewhere and cleaned up the mess because the papers are aligned again in a circle, the two of us in the middle. I don't see him with my real eyes although I know which cushion on the couch he occupies.

"I like where you have taken The Messenger, by the way. A man who wants to die is fearlessly poetic, isn't he?"

I agree. It's nice to bounce plot lines and character details off of one of the characters in the novel. I suppose this is a privilege.

"Of course it is. How many authors write alone? Secluded? James Joyce liked writing in his furnace room because he lost himself in the hum of the motor. Even he needed some sound to keep him company. Hemingway preferred the life sounds of Cuba, God knows why."

I sit crosslegged in the circle of my research trying to find the opening detail for the next chapter. I gave The Messenger a car to travel by but I'm not sure I want him to arrive in Bsharri so quickly.

"Strand him somewhere. Make him find the protagonist on foot, like a lost man on an ironic pilgrimage," The Man from my walk-in closet suggests. He makes a good point. It shouldn't be easy, although The Messenger is travelling in a murder victim's car, gifted to him by the murderer himself, cleaned by the murderer's sons, who so happened to bury the victim in their back-yard, formerly the victim's own backyard.

"You can't let her into the story just yet," The Man hints. He means my wife, although I feel I have already let her in. She knows the story isn't mine, that I stole it.

"She doesn't know who you stole it from. How you took advantage of that situation."

How does he know, The Man from my closet? Obviously he has access to my thoughts. It isn't fair he uses this access against me. I remind him he is my creation.

"All things created are not your own, just borrowed for your convenience, son," he preaches in a condescending manner.

"I have to get back to the story."

"You have to get back to your wife first."

I hit save and nearly kick an opening from the paper circle. Life happens, and as Hemingway used to say, I was out of juice anyway.

Day 5

I find myself head first in a toilet the next hour. For the past six months my stomach has been gurgling like overcooked oil in a frying pan. I never paid it much attention. Mind over matter, or in this case, mind over digestion issues. After cuddling my wife, I couldn't find the peaceful comfort to fall into a deep sleep. My stomach was regurgitating its contents so I descended the stairs searching for a glass of water. Halfway down, I rushed to the basement bathroom to vomit. And I haven't stopped since, losing count after ten. Never thought I held so much in. The story of my life, I suppose. I can't even leave the bathroom for that glass of water. There is a fire alarming an evacuation within and everything is poised to escape through the front door.

The Man keeps me company in this lonely state and I appreciate his silence. He sits on the other side of the toilet without disgust. I realize his expectations for me and my story, and his distaste for digression, but I think he feels sorry for me. He doesn't even joke. In my mind's eye, I can see him staring at me with a friendly face. The way my mother would do before she placed a wet, cool cloth over my forehead. How I missed that nurturing detail after growing up and similar ones like it.

When my stomach finally stalls the exodus of its poison, nausea sets in like a weather pressure movement pressing down. I want it to stop. I beg for it to stop. Nothing like nausea to bring your face to the coldness of a ceramic tile in the basement bathroom. With my cheek on the tile I see those long-legged spiders caught in their own web, possibly dead in their own web. I worry about centipedes exacting their revenge on me. I've killed so many down here. The fast, wormy way they move is reason enough to run for a wad of toilet paper or Kleenex.

The Man disappears after the nausea attacks. I don't see him anywhere, not even in my imagination. I wonder if I vomited out my concern for him and flushed it down the toilet.

My wife finds me barely alive, or at least feeling that way, when the baby gets up for her first feeding in the morning.

"Are you all right?"

"Keep the baby away," I mumble.

"She's upstairs. Do you want me to call in sick for you?"

"No, it's okay."

I try to get up and crawl on hands and knees towards her feet, like that diseased person in the New Testament who solely wants to touch the robe of the Saviour.

"I'm calling you in," she leaves. And I collapse again. All I can think about is not giving it to the kids. I don't want anyone to go through this feeling that won't go away, despite my best efforts to will it away.

And then I think of The Messenger, stranded in my story. I apologize for leaving his journey suspended.

"I didn't see it coming."

My wife is back, though, with my glass of water.

"We never see it coming, honey," she says. "Stay down here. I'll keep the kids upstairs."

She means our spare bed in the basement for guests that never stay over.

The Man is upset with me.

"Don't think you can talk to them too. I'm the only one you can talk to."

He defends his privilege.

"I'm sorry. I promised to write every day."

"He can wait. He's already crossed the border. I'm not sure you want him to nearly die on his way to Bsharri anyway."

"How do you know, I was thinking . . ."

And then I pass out again.

DAY 5 (CONTINUED)

I can't tell if it is day or night in the basement, although I suspect it is raining outside. I can hear it on occasion when a breeze slaps a sheet of drops against the smaller basement windows.

I can also hear footsteps upstairs. My wife's lengthy ones. All of my children. My one-year-old daughter's hurried steps. My five-year-old son's heavy steps. My four-year-old's bull-legged steps, his ankle braces dragging along the floor, up the stairs. He is four but just learning to walk. With Down syndrome, his muscle tone is so low. It is miraculous he can stand up, but he does to our constant praise, which he loves and imitates.

My eldest son is not upstairs. It is mid-week and he is living with his mother four hours away. Every two weeks, I pick him up in London, the mid-point between us. I get him for the weekend and then drive him the same route back on Sunday. It isn't nearly enough time, although it has been our reality for the past ten years.

The Man has disappeared for good, I believe, and I worry I betrayed him by trying to speak directly to my other character, The Messenger. Perhaps I am too polite with my characters. Or maybe, I don't want to hurt their feelings. And the more I think about it, they will surely take advantage of me if I am too nice to them. They are my creations and as such, they need to do my bidding. Not the other way around. What is wrong with speaking to more than one character? The Man doesn't own me. He isn't some Darth Vader type with the secret identity of my biological father hiding behind a ventilated mask. So why do I care either way? I can kill him off if I so choose. It's my story, not his, so he needs to know his place in it.

When you're sick and lying in bed staring at a drop ceiling tile with the light bulb burned out (my wife has been nagging me to change it for as long as I can remember, and go figure, now it is symbolic), you can't help to re-evaluate how you live. Your body turns off but your mind is ready to sign the treaty, make amends, work together again with the flesh to live better, healthier, happier.

I feel guilty my wife has to take care of me when she needs to be taken care of herself. Her footsteps are determined upstairs. I can virtually translate them. Her convicted, 'you kids need to get dressed' footsteps. Her gliding, collecting misshapen toys, footsteps. Her quiet, stoic, at the stove top rooted footsteps. Those heavy, I'll carry the both of you upstairs, footsteps.

The nausea hasn't gone away yet and the only act I am permitted to perform is thinking. I think about the next chapter some more. Where do I take The Messenger before I introduce him to Kashif in Bsharri? Do I stop him in another village? Do I have him pull over on the side of the road to admire the view of higher altitudes in the distance, only to have him run over an Improvised Explosive Device (IED)? That seems a little harsh, but him surviving it only adds to the irony of his life. How he wants to die and how he can't, for the life of him, finally achieve it.

Once again, I worry for his hurt feelings. He might think I am playing with him. I had similar thoughts after feeling the lump in my wife's breast, like I was being played with again by the possibility of another tragedy rolling in.

Or am I misinterpreting tragedy for life, the nature of it. Its remarkable ability to surprise you with a fateful punch from a hidden fist.

I try to force myself up and find myself dizzy again. In front of one of those illusion paintings with no legs or the swivel of a neck to escape. I have to wait it out so my story will have to wait it out with me. The Man is in the darkened room. He agrees. He is not angry, as I suspected. Just patient, like all of my characters, on page or not.

I realize that his loneliness is part of his disguise. Although he created this island for himself, it bores him on most days. He seeks adventures, like all of us. He seeks to know people, to hear about their exploits. But he is far more sophisticated than a Facebook stalker and more complicated. Seeing other people in foreign lands taking selfie shots or recording themselves for the general audience doesn't appeal to him. He desires something homemade with homemade intentions. He wants it from scratch, with love in it.

I communicate my dilemma with him.

"I've reconsidered," he answers.

"Reconsidered what?"

"His unfortunate luck. It defines part of who he is, not all of it, but part of who he is. He managed to cross the border rather easily and the murderer spares him. It's time to balance his luck a little. Remind him what he is up against."

"Which is?"

"His desire to die. Those who want to die, never do. And those who fear it are the first to go."

"So you think I should send him off of a cliff."

"No, he's done that already. He needs to explode, before he pieces himself together again."

"Is that believable to a reader?" I ask The Man.

"Make it believable . . . sip some water first."

I do as I am told and the water feels good in my mouth.

Day 6

I call in sick another day. Still nauseous. Still unable to read, even my own writing. I find my old glasses. I've been squinting through life after I tried contacts two years ago. I think it led to a bout of Bell's Palsy and nearly three months of facial rehabilitation. The stimulation machine vibrating the soft nerves of my face and some pretty painful acupuncture fixed the frozen nerves, except for when I smile. My left eye closes entirely, like it is swollen from a punch.

Three of my kids are at school and my baby daughter is happy I am home. She locates me downstairs with a mischievous smile. She slaps my face to wake me up. She finds it funny that someone is sleeping on her awake time.

The sight of her face gets me up on my feet but my legs are weaker and I have lost weight. This I can feel.

My mother is upstairs when I come up.

"What is wrong with you? I didn't know. You guys don't call."

My mother has her own health issues, not to mention nursing my father, who found himself in a wheelchair after a closed brain injury and some doctor malpractice. I try my best not to need her. She often reminds me that you can never eliminate this connection.

"I'll be all right."

My daughter reaches for me to pick her up and everyone in the room, including my wife, stare at me wondering what decision I am about to make. They know how particular I am about these things, about protecting my daughter from my germs.

"Not now, sweetie," I answer her. She runs off to draw attention to her independence before playing with a dolphin toy.

"You need to take more days off, take care of yourself," my mother preaches.

"He does. He takes care of himself."

My wife feels the need to defend me, although she knows I've been spending late nights writing. My mother suspects I am lying. She too, more so than my wife, sees no value in sacrificing your health for the possibility of publication. Especially with no monetary reward at the end of the sacrifice. My parents are immigrants. They worked hard so that we could have "clean" jobs. Creating additional work or stress for yourself is counter productive to their American Dream, except they often forget we live in Canada.

I return to the basement and collapse onto the bed again. The pillows have cooled and they renew my faith in feeling better. I fall in and out of sleep, in between Tylenol dreams, and then I wake up to an idea before I realize—I need to be better.

Day 6 (continued)

With one foot out of the basement of my sickness, I find a crayon downstairs and locate The Messenger on a journal page waiting to descend a road into a pine shaded valley. I discover him abandoned in the story, alone, although content in his temporary suspension. The Man in my story jokes in my mind's ear that I did The Messenger a favour by not writing him out. He says I gave him some time to think before his next adventure. Instead, I am surprised by The Messenger's quiet perseverance. I see him as someone willing to wait to be written correctly and in this context I use him as an example to The Man.

"Why can't you be more like him?"

"I stood by you when you were sick, didn't I?"

I can't complain so I decide to write something out of the ordinary pattern of The Messenger's life. I decide to make him happy for a moment.

I realize The Messenger would despise any notion of happiness. However, his body's reaction to the old cedars and the crisp air entering the car from a rolled down window allow him to breathe with a smile on his face.

He is not accustomed to feeling good about himself. He expected much more frustration crossing the border of Syria into North Lebanon. He anticipated injury, outright rejection and maybe an abusive deportment. He encountered neither. If anything, the accomplishment of his plan justified an acceptance of success or something going right for once in his life.

His descent into the valley is steep and he is distracted by the aesthetic beauty of his surroundings, which resemble those hiking days from his youthful years in Canada. He had visited Lebanon many times before, in a working capacity, but never did his former life's career provide him the opportunity of wandering or exploring his surroundings without purpose. In the present, he considers himself beyond a reliance on time. This newfound patience inspires the wisdom of appreciating his immediate surroundings with an artist's sensitivity. The rocky cliffs interrupted by blankets of wooden green offer him serenity. He thinks about his message and the mission wrapped within it. It would come as a surprise to this mysterious man named Kashif. And the surprise would inspire retaliation, which, to his personal benefit, would mean his salvation.

The Messenger is hungry and the smell of smoke with the spice of burning meat from a mysterious source in the distance only intensifies the growling in his stomach.

(I try my best to avoid the introduction of any type of food myself, but the thought of it no longer turns my stomach. If anything, I begin to fantasize about food when I realize that The Messenger, like the author creating him, needs to eat. He shared a drink with the murderer in Kaa. Now he craves a taste of the land.)

He looks at the gauge and realizes he has been driving on empty for quite some time. He doesn't care about running out of gas. He enjoys his patience with death. In the past, he could argue he rushed the majority of his suicide attempts. Now he finds sacred the epiphany to simplify his needs. The option of letting death come to him, instead, secures. He had chased it so violently after his son's death. Perhaps he tried too hard to die afterwards, scaring the fate part of it away. With the assurance of The Man lending him faith it would happen without a doubt this time, he prepares himself for a poetic end. This time around, he respects the pacing of death creeping up to him slowly, like the disease that skipped over him to attack his first born after depleting the life out of his wife—literally.

When he reaches the bottom of the valley, he can feel in the pedal that he won't have enough gas to make it up another hill and over the peak of another mountain. So he rides the car along the gravel shoulder only to have a tire pop as it halts to a stop.

He abandons the car and decides to follow the scent of invisible smoke. After he takes a step towards it, he hears the loading of a weapon. It isn't the sound of a war rifle, but one of a hunter. He can't see the man about to shoot him until he notices a young boy cocking the rifle to his head.

"Sssh," the boy says.

The Messenger remains still and then the gun goes off. Whatever is dead behind him purrs, its stomach gurgling, sickening with the ingestion of its own blood. And to The Messenger's surprise, it isn't an animal he expects to see in one of these remote valleys before the mountainous Bsharri region. By this point the boy has dropped the gun. He is tanned with black hair and black eyes. He kneels beside the dying tiger and makes the sign of the cross.

Day 7

The Messenger doesn't know where he is. Without a map, he drove the murdered victim's car in a north east direction. Towards the white caps. Or, *milk peaks* as they were once labelled by a visiting artist in my research notes. Now he watches a young village boy pray over a dying tiger.

He considers the surreal nature of this scene. He walks over to the child, whose eyes remain closed and tight. His gunpowder-stained fingers are interlocked. His dry skinned elbows are parallel to the weedy ground. The tiger is breathing still. Friendly as it dies. Humble to be taken down by a mere child with expert aim. Its eyes are sapphire green. Its fur rust orange with black stripes. The Messenger wonders if its family is lurking in the bush, creating a circle of fire. Although he appreciates the act of dying, he never imagined himself torn apart by a vicious predator in any of his death dreams. The young boy reveals no panic in his prayerful kneeling posture. He is staunch erect and not resting his backside on his ankles. When the prayer ends to awaken him, he pets the tiger's fur. The tiger appreciates the softness of this child's hand. The child's hand disappears at times under the majesty of the striped fur before reappearing to straighten out any ruffles.

The tiger purrs. The tiger purrs. The tiger licks the stale fur around its mouth and then the tiger purrs again.

The Messenger steps closer. The boy is not afraid of The Messenger, this stranger recently stranded on the side of the road. He continues to pet the predator as if rewarding it for being housebroken by a bullet.

There is no need to ask questions while the tiger struggles to breathe against the red spot on his chest, expanding its wetness. A clean, centered shot seems to have partially clipped its heart. Just enough accuracy to soften the suffering.

But the tiger is not suffering. He, or she, is peaceful, relaxed, in a Yoga sequence. The boy refuses to pay The Messenger any attention. His focus remains with the tiger. His petting matches the consistency of the tiger's purring. Both follow the grain of the stripes.

As the tiger lies comfortably on the silty soil, I can't help but stop and think about my research regarding tiger poaching. The Messenger is unaware of this research and I feel like I don't need to inform him of it, especially since this process of dying has already entranced him. But it isn't uncommon to hunt tigers, although there is a hidden reason why the boy shoots it. For years, the tiger has been hunted as a status symbol, its fur often preserved for decorative items such as wall and floor coverings, its blood used in traditional Asian medicines. Not to mention sport and poaching, often extended into illegal trading of tiger parts, such as tiger teeth. In my research, I came across a story where a hunted tiger was traded for a child, like payment for an adoption.

Unlike these scenarios, the boy does not act like a procurer of any of these tradeable options. His hand moves towards the tiger's mouth. Blood has outlined the white fur around it now, matting it down like a gelled beard.

The Messenger finally finds some words in the boy's language.

"Is he yours?"

"He is from the zoo. They left him here after they moved the animals."

"Why?"

"To spite those people who wouldn't pay to see it."

The tiger purrs and The Messenger admires the peace in its rhythmic breaths. The boy shushes the tiger. Its lungs pump its skin into hyperventilation. The boy shushes the tiger some more until it stops breathing with its eyes open. The Messenger shivers. His own dream is to die with his eyes open.

The boy stands and makes the sign of the cross again. He then turns to The Messenger.

"Can you help me carry her?"

"Let us make a stretcher," The Messenger recommends. He points to some loose timber fallen and brittle on the ground. Very quietly, they collect a number of branches. The boy strips some thinner stems that bend and ties the branches at the ends. The Messenger is impressed by the boy's scout skills. He looks no older than seven years.

Once the stretcher is tied, The Messenger and the boy roll the bloodied tiger onto its plank.

"Where are we taking her?"

"Down the hill."

The boy points to a descent of trees. In the distance a line of silver smoke rises like a sharpened blade.

"She doesn't deserve to rot into this lonely soil," the boy explains.

The Messenger grabs one end but worries it is too heavy on the other side when the angle shifts to climb down the hill. So he recommends bearing the bottom side. The boy doesn't refuse the request. He tucks his gun aside the tiger's back and The Messenger follows his nose to the smoke.

The scent of the brush is fresh cedar and vitamin—planting soil. He can feel its blackened, quicksand softness beneath his feet, its dark density in his imagination. These trees thrive on this slope until they transform into apple trees. A tiger and a plot of apple trees. The Messenger questions the possibility of hallucinations inspired by his hunger and thirst. The boy is too friendly a hunter. The tiger is too friendly a predator. The apple trees are too biblical to find a place amongst the history of old cedars. Is he asleep in his consciousness? Is he alive or already in the transition towards death? He had read a short story in a Swedish magazine about a man halfway to death in the midst of a great success in his life. He could feel his breath leaving him as he accepts an award. He fights his legs giving out on him when he glances at the beautiful woman who has promised him her love. And then, just as he is about to fall asleep and accept the good in his life, his arm tightens and his heart stops. The irony of dying in the midst of truly living. Perhaps he is dying, The Messenger considers, before his body's sensory functions detect the catalyst creating it?

"Please slow down, I am losing grip," the boy asks.

The Messenger realizes the steeper slope of the hill is increasing his foot speed.

"I'm sorry."

"I don't want her to fall."

The boy is very respectful of the corpse. This isn't a trophy killing, The Messenger concludes. The boy seems regretful of his kill, like a hunter written in a Hemingway story. He displays no pride in taking down Goliath with his sawed off slingshot of a gun. This is a duty or a promise against his will fulfilled.

When The Messenger reaches level ground, the boy walks horizontal to him and together they walk in a line towards a tiny little rock cabin. The fire outside is healthy and a woman kneads dough on a rock. She rolls it over and over onto itself. She wears a scarf to hold in the colour of her hair. She is younger than The Messenger first judges. This mother, this boy who is her son, the absence of a man, a dead tiger on a makeshift funeral pyre.

She notices him before a formal introduction. She is not threatened by his strangeness. When she sees the tiger in between them, she leaves her work. Her hands are powdered white to her forearms, where the darkened, olive skin begins again.

She pets the fur like her son. Affectionately.

"Are you hungry?"

Her question is directed to The Messenger.

He nods.

"We will not eat her."

Without the need for a cue, the boy opens a trap door to an underground cellar or holding place. Perhaps the crawlspace below the cabin. As if in twos from the ark, animals obediently walk up stairs. Chickens, goats, pigs, sheep, mountain cats. They scatter the immediate grounds with no intent to escape. A few dogs smell the tiger's blood. They test it with a lick before sniffing other areas. The boy shoos them away.

"We will eat in peace, now," the lady says.

The Messenger is thirsty but he is not prepared to ask for anything. The woman returns to the bread she kneads and places it in a stone oven, fire burning on the inside edges. On a spit, a tiny pig is charring black. The boy turns it and The Messenger helps him from the other side.

The Messenger enjoys their silence. The way they both communicate with their bodies, using words only when necessary. Before long, the bread is baked to a hardened crust and the boy carves bubbling meat beneath the crispy skin surface of the burning pig.

They eat outside in silence. In a silence so serene even the farm animals respect it without noise.

The woman is a dainty eater. She picks at the meat and prefers the green dandelion stems salted in a bowl. She eats this delicacy with the warm bread. Famished, the Messenger and the boy share the meat. They share water from a wooden bucket.

"Where am I?" The Messenger asks.

"The wood." The woman smiles. She is being sarcastic.

"You go to Bsharri?" The boy guesses.

"Yes."

"The Poet's home?"

"Yes."

"He made paintings here."

The Messenger is familiar with the Gibran drawings. Biblical, nudes, organic.

"Why did you shoot the tiger?"

The boy looks to his mother to ask permission to explain. The mother nods.

"She terrorized our home. She ate our animals because she was hungry. She growled in the night to remind us she could kill. She tried to make deals with us. Her stomach would never fill."

"We know her stomach would never fill," the mother agrees.

"What zoo gave her freedom?"

"The one that went bankrupt in Bsharri. A rich man's zoo with a trick," the mother explains. "When he ran out of money, he left the killers behind."

"Why?"

"To disrupt our peace, why else?" the boy makes the connection. He seems annoyed by The Messenger's questions now.

"What will you do with it?"

"Bury it in our garden. It doesn't deserve to be eaten."

"Why not?"

"It's not her fault she is hungry."

The Messenger finally understands. After he eats, the boy calls him on to follow. They walk by the tiger. Green flies violently bounce from its head. They dig a hole in the softer soil by the apple orchard. They then drag the tiger's body to the hole. It doesn't seem right to cover such beautiful fur with black soil but The Messenger doesn't have any more questions. Afterwards, the boy climbs some trees to pick some cleaner apples. In his arms, he delivers them to the stone stove. He places them inside and they soften the air with a sweeter scent.

They eat the baked apples and The Messenger is happy again. Everything is so simple here, he thinks. You don't even have to say anything. It is life and death. It is love and apples. It is a breathing poem with a heartbeat and a silent philosophy.

At dusk, The Messenger leaves when he feels the desire to kiss the woman.

Day 8

On my way to London, The Man from my preface argues with me over the last chapter. I am going to pick up my son, as I always do every two weeks. He is my first born from my first marriage. I met my former wife while I did my M.A. in Windsor. She is a poet and of Lebanese descent. She currently lives in Leamington and although we share custody, she maintains residence. So the distance between us is London now, the cut off at Dorchester, exit number 199—the truck stop. For ten years I have been making this trip. The Man doesn't care to disrupt the journey. His sole concern is the story.

"You missed some important details and opportunities in the last chapter," he says.

I ignore him at first. I miss my son and the drive is longer now that it gets darker earlier. Once again, I intimate how the story is mine to design. The Man does make a few good points.

"You forgot to mention that The Messenger was still wearing the border man's uniform. This is important, no? The boy respects him because of this uniform, and the lady trusts him after seeing him with her son and the dead tiger."

"You're right," I admit, but more to pacify him. He goes on.

"Plus, you should have done something a little more dramatic at the end of the chapter. You should have had the boy cut off a paw, or something."

"What would The Messenger do with a real tiger's paw."

"It could have been symbolic down the road in the story. Who knows what it could mean."

"It doesn't work that way," I explain to The Man. "Sometimes, you have to let the story come to you. I can always address it in a rewrite, so there is no cause for concern or emergency. But I didn't want such a bloody symbol to dominate the scene. I wanted to show how The Messenger is melting from his grief. He lost his wife and soul mate, he lost his son, so he has turned off everything except his desire to die. In doing so, he has made himself frozen to human interaction, or a step further, he refuses to engage. Seeing the beautiful mother with her head scarf in the role of taking care of her son, all alone, appeals to The Messenger. And he leaves, rather stealthily, when he begins to feel a physical attraction to her. It makes him feel guilty, like he is not honouring his wife's memory, or his son's for that matter. So he leaves. He removes himself and escapes before he can confront the faint desire to live again."

The Man is quiet after I explain this motivation. He had lost focus of The Messenger's character in place of the visual. I suppose The Man is a visual learner, like some of my lower level readers at school, except he is much more manipulative and old school clever. After I explain to him my thought process, I wonder if he is taking notes on me, observing my tactics, so as to learn where this story is heading, even before it comes to me.

So I stop. And I resolve within myself to stay the course of unpredictability and suspense, now that I have a secret spy watchdog on my ass.

When I reach the truck stop my son is waiting inside with his mother and her parents. They help raise him and sometimes my son spends more time under their care than hers. I can tell right away that my former wife needs to tell me something.

She rarely speaks "to" me and our conversations often stay within the envelope of our mutual interest in our son. This time around, there is something disturbing her beyond the caution line.

"I got a call from his teacher."

I look to my eleven-year-old son. He turns away and rolls his eyes before burying his hands in his pockets. He needs a haircut desperately and his belly has grown to protrude over his waistline.

"What did he say?"

I ask this question with a feigned angry frown for my son. He is still looking away.

"He is disruptive in class. Like a class clown, and disrespectful sometimes. He's like that a home too. His marks have dropped. At hockey he skips drills."

"Is this all true?"

My son nods. He is always embarrassed when we speak about him in front of him.

"He's a mean teacher. I didn't do anything. He asked about "clubs" and I said the "Caboto Club" and everyone laughed but he didn't laugh. He meant like, drama club, or the chess club, and not a social club."

"I know that isn't everything," I say. My son is clever and he has already exploited the spaces in his parents' dysfunctional relationship to secure him the privileges of lying.

"I have no confidence, Daddy," he says.

My former wife raises her eyebrows. I try my best not to cry in front of my son. What eleven-year-old says he has no confidence? He is a bright kid who has performed admirably in school. He is an avid reader. Over the summer he finished The Harry Potter series in one month to win a bet with me, and now he has no confidence, just a few months later.

"We're going to talk. Get in the truck," I point, and he walks, dejected, on his own. All I can think about is how sorry I feel for him. I try my best to disguise it with my anger. I have to be a father now, and the bad guy, and although I don't like this role, and I would rather be the teacher, or the Dad who shows him how to be a man, I understand our limitations. It's hard to father him over the phone. It's hard when you find yourself three hours away to intercede on a "live" menial ritual like finishing your homework.

He sits in the front seat now.

"Disrespectful?" I raise my voice as I start the truck. It rumbles to back up my voice. He doesn't say anything.

"That's what you are? Disrespectful? My son is disrespectful?" I'm borderline losing my temper. My flu stomach gurgles and I worry I may lose something the other way, in my pants. I tighten my gut.

"We're going to fix this."

I lay into him for nearly an hour on the drive back. I grill him with questions, why he isn't paying attention in class, why he is staying up at night, why he isn't eating properly. (I face-timed him recently to see a 7-11 Slurpee in the frame of the screen.)

As I'm giving it to my son, like The Man was giving it to me prior, I am recording where I see a potential deficiency in my parenting. My former wife tries her best as a single mother, and so do her parents, but the arrow keeps stopping at me and my absence in his life.

My son is trying to force himself to cry now to make me stop. I end my admonishment in style:

"That's it. Look at the sign. We hit Hamilton. You're lucky it didn't last the whole drive."

In the aftermath, he apologizes to me. He makes his promises to change. He isn't an addict or an alcoholic, but I worry about his future without my surveillance. I suppose, as an author, I am accustomed to keeping control of a story, but his story is as unpredictable as the one I am working on. And maybe this isn't so bad. Maybe he needs to find himself in the chaos just like my characters, just like their author.

"I just want you to feel good about yourself, to dream and believe you can be what you imagine yourself to be. You think your Daddy likes to yell at you? It breaks my heart one thousand times more when I see yours breaking."

He stares at me for an awkward length. I review what I said to him hoping I didn't cuss as I did so.

"How much time until we get home?"

"Under an hour."

"Do you mind if I sleep a little."

When he closes his eyes, I let myself cry in the darkness of the truck. The Man is nowhere to be found and I worry he has seen my greatest weakness.

Day 8 (Later that night)

The upcoming chapter I am trying to write is often interrupt-ed by bouts of stomach cramps and trips to the toilet. After returning home and tucking in my son with a traitor's kiss, my gurgling stomach forces me to isolate myself in the basement again. I can't sleep. My stomach is upset and I worry I have food poisoning now.

With no hope of a peaceful rest in sight, I relocate The Messenger hitchhiking at night, just past where he abandoned his car.

Although it is dusk, there is a red laser line tracing the white peaks in the distance. To The Messenger, it resembles a Pink Floyd album cover, Dark Side of the Moon. The Messenger is not afraid to be hitchhiking. He is well fed and relaxed. And the walk up a steeper slope is a soft one on gravel. It doesn't take long for a metallic green four-door sedan to pull up ahead of him. The Messenger chases the red brake lights and hurries to the passenger side door.

"Bsharri?" the younger man in a suit and tie asks. The inside of the car smells like mint trapped in an artificial package.

"Yes."

"Get in, soldier."

The Messenger remembers what he is wearing now. The customs official's uniform. It must have been his lawful uniform which prompted this professionally clad man to stop his vehicle. The Messenger doesn't respond to the acknowledgment. If the uniform protects him, he achieves his mission faster by reaching Bsharri on schedule.

The younger professional is very careful as he pulls back onto the road. He uses his directional signal, before he merges quickly into the passing traffic.

The vehicle itself is newer, leather seats covered in custom plastic sheaths. Every time The Messenger moves, he hears himself doing so.

"It is a new car. I asked for the covers. I know, covering the dash and where your feet rest is a little much."

"It is very clean," The Messenger agrees, forcing a complimentary tone of voice.

"My name is Sifar."

"I would like to tell you my name, but I am not permitted to do so, under any circumstances."

The Messenger presents this requirement of his mission as he would a joke, the punchline being no need to worry with a man in uniform. With the armoured support of the uniform, The Messenger does not feel rude in saying this. He feels Sifar will understand.

"I thought of becoming an official myself. Actually, I nearly joined the army."

"What prevented you?"

"Education, the Civil War, hypocrisy."

The latter term ruffles his skin as he says it. He squirms in his plastic sheathed seat. It sounds as if he is stretching the car from the inside out so he can fit his legs into it better.

"Are you a fence man, like the rest of them?"

This question is rather aggressive for The Messenger.

"A fence man?"

"Yes. At the border. A secret Sunni in uniform, letting Syrian rebels across."

The Messenger considers admitting his identity honestly. His military uniform seems to be communicating messages he can't necessarily control.

"I do not know what you mean."

The Messenger settles on ignorance instead. It is, he decides, safer to pretend you know nothing about who you are pretending to be.

Sifar is agitated. He loosens his tie with a violent tug. The plastic surrounding him reacts with a warping sound. The Messenger remains as still as he can.

"I suppose killings and kidnappings don't mean anything to you, or the Cedar Revolution. How soon we forget."

Although his former life's position as peacekeeper on the U.N. interim force introduced these ongoing clashes between Sunni opposition forces and Lebanese Armed Forces, his outside peacekeeping role prevented him from realizing the deeper roots of conflict on the border of Syria and Lebanon.

"I work as any man does in uniform," The Messenger says. He knows diffusing a situation involves humility and concession.

"Yeah, you work all right, for both sides of the fence."

"I can walk the rest of the way, if you prefer?"

The Messenger decides that Sifar's tone of voice is far from compromise or casual discussion. He is speeding now and his one hand is trembling on the steering wheel. This turn of events has happened so fast. This violent metamorphosis between man in suit and angry protestor yielded no hint or gun powder line. Just three seconds, like a grenade, and detonation.

As the car ascends the hill, The Messenger sees a straight line of clouds replacing the red line. A very straight, thin sheet of clouds stretching from one end of the earth to the other, like an equator in the sky.

"How about you die the rest of the way." These words explode from Sifar's ballooned cheeks like a sudden burst of steam. He yanks the car over to the side and before The Messenger expects it, this man who is dressed for a funeral is stabbing him violently with a knife of no bulging origin. The Messenger feels it plunging into his abdomen, and then into his chest; he feels it missing his neck as he instinctively pushes the door open. The man kicks him out of the car. While The Messenger waits for Sifar to jump out himself and finish the job, he understands the symbolism of the plastic sheathed interior now.

As expected, Sifar jumps out with no hurry. He shuffles sand into dust clouds as he stands over and spits on The Messenger.

"One less traitor to this country is one more blessing for peace."

The Messenger struggles to find his bleeding wounds with his hands. He can feel the warmth of his blood leaving his body, in between his fingers. He can also feel the warmth of this man's spit on his face, cooling quickly.

Just as he imagined every time he tried to kill himself, twenty-three times and counting, his life presents visuals in this flushing of blood transition to the other side. He sees the woman in the scarf and her tiny son, the tiger killer, crouching in the darkness of the bushes. He imagines them watching him die, as he imagines his own son and wife in another lifetime. His wife is breastfeeding his newborn son in the shadow of moonlight seeping in from the half blinded window. Her golden hair is aglow as is a spot on his son's smooth face. It is one of the scenes which haunts him as a motif, recurring with additional details to colour and reflect its meaning.

Before Sifar leaves his position in the sky to enter his car again, The Messenger chokes.

"Thank you," he says.

The car speeds off leaving a sheath of gravel that settles on him like tiny hail pellets, or the first shovel of dirt in a grave.

The Messenger has finally achieved his wish despite the incompletion of his mission. He will die with a beautiful view of the night sky and the thin clouds moving rapidly against a backdrop of stars and falling flashing lights. He had always wondered what those floating, flashing lights were. Were they airplanes, or helicopters, or satellites posing as falling stars? Nonetheless, they are as beautiful as the stars themselves, and not trapped in a static constellation.

DAY 9

My middle son finds me passed out in the bathroom, like they did Elvis Presley. Hunched over my knees on the toilet with nothing left to give. My laptop out of battery on the hamper I used as a desk.

"What are you doing, Daddy?"

"Dying?"

"But you're still alive."

This is my son, Oscar, my second born, who is ironically blonde with ebony eyes. He is wearing his new glasses. We have finally sold him on them.

"I know. Can you turn around so that Daddy can pull up his pants?"

"Privacy?"

"Yes, privacy, good boy."

Another remembered lesson apparently learned.

I worry if I saved the last segment before I passed out. Luckily for me, I recall the technology of auto save, which saves me another panic-induced toilet episode. Nothing like losing something you wrote. Instant horror.

When my son leaves to give me privacy, The Man enters to occupy it.

"You killed him before the mission? Now we have to start all over again, find someone new to send my message? I don't get it. I don't get you. Kashif was supposed to kill him after he received the message, like passing a simple baton. You did this on purpose to spite me."

I don't answer him. I hobble to the sink to wash my hands and to see two sunken eye sockets traced in charcoal. Except, there is no energy in these sun blockers, only fatigue.

"If he dies, he dies," I recite this famous '80s movie line under my breath to intimidate The Man. He is not impressed by my allusive humour.

"He was worthy enough to deliver the message and you know it."

I don't respond. I can hear footsteps all over the floor above. The heaven of my family awaking too early in the morning to beat the sun with breakfast activity.

I remove the laptop from the bathroom for fear one of my younger children will find a place for it in the toilet (perhaps where it belongs), and store it instead on a bookshelf. I need to spend the day talking to my eldest son. He needs to know how much I care about him. Like a miracle worker, I actually believe I can convert him back to confidence.

My wife is making waffles for my son Tobias, whose diet is very limited due to his aversion to textures—another side effect of being Downs. He loves waffles and dipping them in syrup. His only other preference is ice cream. He can eat ice cream any time of his waking day, and yours, and anyone else's in the vicinity. He is an ice cream addict, like his mom and dad.

The waffle batter smell doesn't help my stomach in the least. I resolve to return to my flu water diet, except my right eye is really sore for some reason. Perhaps I threw up one too many times, or maybe it is a sinus thing. Whatever it is, my wife notices me in pieces.

"Boy, you look like you are falling apart."

"Thanks. Is Aidan up yet?"

"No. Everything all right with him?"

"He's not getting along with his teacher and he's been disrespectful. His grades have dropped."

"Oh my."

I can tell she is distracted in her tone of voice. She went in for her mammogram and we are awaiting the tests in the torture of real life suspense. Leave it to doctors to have mastered the art of it.

"I want him to come and live with us, full time," I say, not in the form of a question.

"I think he needs you too," she says, as if interpreting my real intentions.

Before I can answer her, I have to rush to the bathroom again. However, this is a dud run. When I arrive at the toilet, I realize I have nothing left in my stomach to throw up again. Not even bile. The Man is waiting for me in this bathroom too. My kids are outside the door, knocking wildly to enter. Even Oscar, whom I thought learned the value of privacy.

"I know what you are doing with The Messenger. I figured it out. Like On The Sidewalk Bleeding."

This scares me. He can read my thoughts.

"You want him to realize there is a reason to live before he actually dies. You wouldn't have spent so much time and words leading him to Bsharri, just to let him die just outside of it. You're not that masochistic."

Once again, I wash my face in this upstairs sink. The dimmer lighting is more flattering to my paler complexion. I haven't shaved in a week either and there are hairs growing everywhere. Just below my eyes, on my temples, my ears. I need to recover my neglected self.

I ignore The Man but he continues.

"You liked that story as a kid, didn't you?"

He is alluding to "On The Sidewalk Bleeding," a story about a young, teenaged gang member who gets ambushed when he leaves a party to buy some smokes. It is raining and he can't speak, but he tries desperately to die without his gang jacket. He struggles to remove it. In the meantime, three parties of people discover him but are too afraid to help. He manages to get the jacket off, but by the end of the story, when the police officer is writing the report, he notices the discarded jacket first. He says, "just another Royal," and Andy's dream of dying as himself, as just Andy, is tragically destroyed.

I received the strap, or actually, the ruler strap, in grade six for reading the story. I had finished my homework and Mr. Hill, our six-foot-five Iroquois Indian English teacher, had ventured to the back of the classroom from his permanent position of writing terms on the blackboard. After finishing early, I opened my desk and found the grade eight book of stories, the last of which was "On the Sidewalk Bleeding." As I finished reading it, he was staring over me. He called me to the front of the class and sarcastically gave me the ruler on my hand, in front of Christine Persia, a girl I was hopelessly in love with. I kept telling myself, "don't cry, don't cry" because I didn't want her to see me cry. She would never like me if she saw me cry.

I remember going home and telling my mom, and in her Italian immigrant way she said I deserved it.

From that moment on, the story, "On The Sidewalk Bleeding" seemed to follow me. As a teacher, I found it surviving the cuts into new story anthologies. I taught it so many times that I decided to write a gang story myself. My story published under the title "Blood Relatives." When I read it at the magazine launch, an elderly woman in the front row approached me afterwards. She said my story reminded her of a story she used to teach. At the same time we said, "On The Sidewalk Bleeding," and the irony was finally complete.

I received a nomination for The Journey Prize for that story, but it didn't make the shortlist.

Although I hadn't purposely tried to put The Messenger in the same predicament, I found myself later in the day, as I watched my children take swimming lessons at the university pool, wondering if my subconscious managed to put The Messenger "On The Hill Bleeding." The Man must have secured access to my subconscious a step before it dictated the words to my fingers. This worried me. I didn't want him to interfere with the story. He was just a character. He didn't have the rights or authorial privileges, and yet, he was clever enough to see influence in my work.

My eldest son stays a safe distance away from me the entire Saturday. He hides in the group of his brothers and sister, or with those who visit to see him. I can tell he doesn't want to talk about his troubles any more. He doesn't appreciate my disappointment in him. This time, I made a hurtful impression and I begin to feel guilty again for hurting his feelings. I have to convince myself to stay strong to my words. I am his father, a parent, in a position of authority (as I assume I am with my novel), but instinctively drawn to hug and kiss him. My embattled Italian grandmother on my father's side, the one who never visited a hospital, and died at 93, the same one who walked ten miles a day in the harsh Canadian winter with grocery bags creasing her veiny hands, used to tell my father that you kiss your kids when they are asleep—so that you don't make them weak to a cruel world. Although I considered this advice heartless at one point in my life, I reconsidered its rationale in the context of my fatherly responsibilities. It just felt unfair to attack him, when he spent so much time away from me.

So I made him confess to everyone in our extended family so that he wouldn't develop the habit of hiding things from me.

He hated me for making him expose himself with honesty, all of the stuff that contributed to this lack of confidence, but by the end of this exercise, we were both laughing at it. I think it made him feel like he was big enough to defeat it. We watched the hockey game together at night, and fell asleep together on the couch.

Day 10

Blasted out of bed by a bright, blinding, early morning sun storm, I sneak downstairs again to the kitchen before the kids wake. On the page, I find my dying Messenger, stranded on a hill, bleeding into the sand, physically absorbing into the night. Except, when I try to locate my notes for the next chapter (I usually type them in before erasing them when I start writing again), his perilous future disappears.

I never leave a day's work without reviewing my notes for the next instalment, and yet, these notes disappear, and with them, so does the fate of my Messenger. Notes cannot find the delete button on their own. Or did someone not like what he saw.

The Man's attempt at a subtle hint only serves to annoy me. The Man must have infiltrated my laptop and erased the direction I was heading in, although little does he know I often deviate from it anyway.

I have no intention of killing The Messenger. I never did. And contrary to what The Man assumed or predicted, I don't want him to end up like Andy in the short story, "On The Sidewalk Bleeding." I don't want him to die this death, despite The Messenger's insatiable and ironic desire to die by another's hand.

So I begin the next chapter by placing him in the brightness of sunlight breaking into a hospital room. When his eyes open, The Messenger believes himself in Heaven or at least a bright purgatory before it. It makes him feel good again to feel new, resurrected life, to realize the afterlife is not a deep, historic sleep. All he can see is light when he opens his eyes. No shapes or shadows yet. Just light. The warmth of it heating his skin embalms his lips. In his heart, he feels overjoyed to have escaped the torture of his previous, natural life. All of the tragedy, the string of misfortune cut and re-stitched with stronger knots to make it more difficult with pulling to untie and loosen. The loss of his wife. The loss of his son. Each and every attempt at suicide. The strange, coincidental salvations.

This is the immortality he craved. A lighted one.

He could sense water sliding down his cheek from his eyes, sticking and pooling in the spaces between his neck and shoulders. A cleansing of flesh water to be replaced and dried by the bright light.

And then the voice.

"You are waking."

He had heard this voice before. In his previous life. It continues.

"Do you see me, yet?"

The Messenger squints and more water flushes from his eyes. Sparkles appear in the light to replace the blurriness and deaden the brightness. A shadow behind the translucent shower curtain of light grows larger and develops an outline of edges. The Messenger can now smell the man's skin, an alcohol-based pungent scent creeping in from the left side, where this man's hand checks the pulse on his neck.

"What is your name?"

The Messenger doesn't feel like he can talk. Does he have a name, anymore? Is it relevant in this other world?

"Can you see me, sir?"

The Messenger keeps squinting. The voice is insistent. As blurry as the light preventing him from sharpening the focus of his eyes.

He squints one last time. When his eyelids open, he sees a nose very close to his. The face reverses.

"We almost lost you. I mean, what am I saying, I tried to lose you."

An evil giggle accompanies a familiar accent.

The Messenger squints again, repeatedly, like something is caught in his eye. And the more he tries to see, the more blind the water in his eyes makes him. His hands are restrained to steel bars. What Heaven is this? He panics. "I can't move my legs, either."

He struggles to see until he gives up and refuses the exercise.

He falls asleep.

When he awakens, a man whom he recognizes is sitting at the edge of his bed. This man is wearing a white lab coat. It is no longer bright in the room, but dark up above, with subtle fluorescent under lighting creating a glow from below.

"Am I above the clouds?" The Messenger asks.

"No, you are below them."

"Why are you here?"

"I saved you from your wounds."

"I am not alive."

"Yes, you are."

"You didn't save me."

"Yes, I did."

"You were the one who tried to kill me."

"Also correct."

"This cannot be."

"But it is."

"What are you doing to me?"

"Nothing I haven't done to anyone else."

"Which is?"

"Kill and save them at the same time."

"Why?"

"I have my reasons."

"I want to die. Kill me again."

"I can't do that."

"Why?"

"It doesn't work that way."

"How does it work?"

"You live now, that's all, until you die again."

The words make The Messenger feel sleepy so he drifts away with the hope of never waking to the same nightmare—Sifar, his murderer, is dressed as a doctor.

It is Sunday, and after I finish my chapter for the day, my kids wake up on cue—for the first time in our family history.

They charge downstairs with hungry eyes. It is still sunny and the glare is making Aidan squint.

"What would you like for breakfast, buddy?"

"I'm not hungry yet. Oh, nothing now please."

Once again, I feel sorry after realizing his effort to sound more polite. He is trying hard to get on my better side.

"You are coming with me today."

"I know, you drive me back today, Daddy."

"No, we are going to church and then I am taking you for a haircut. We are going to stop into the bookstore and I am going to buy you a book. But first you are going to write a letter."

"A letter? Why?"

"Because it's the right thing to do?"

"Like a real letter?"

"Yes."

"To whom?"

"Your teacher."

He hates this idea. He blows air from his mouth and leans back.

"Are you pouting now?"

"No. Why am I writing *him* a letter?"

"To apologize, and to show him you are better than what he believes you to be."

"What is the letter going to do?"

"Show him you are serious about changing your behaviour in his class. It's like a contract and he can hold it to you because it's on paper. Like a written promise."

I can tell my wife, who is currently making waffle batter for Tobias, is impressed by the idea. She nods her head.

It's the best idea I could think of before I drive almost four hours away to talk to this teacher in person. At the very least, my son doesn't expect it, and I can exploit a teachable moment, shrinking away with the fact I have to drive him back to London in a couple of hours.

"He won't like it."

"Yes, he will."

"What do you want me to write?"

"What you know you need to do, that's all. Put it on paper and make it real."

I hear the echo in my voice the more I talk. It seems like I am talking about my own writing, and furthermore, what I believe about the written word.

Aidan reluctantly grabs a piece of paper from the computer printer and I hand him my nice pen.

"Address it properly, like a professional. It will make him believe you are serious."

He does as I ask and before long he has a list of errors he promises to repudiate.

"Now, you are going to type it out. You are going to give him the rough draft and a good draft. And you are going to sign it at the bottom."

He follows the instructions and produces the final copy to me. I add a note, myself, to ensure the teacher gets it. I don't want my son to throw away the letter or pretend to lose it.

"I want this in your knapsack tonight. I'm going to tell your mother at the drop off."

He pouts before finding a distraction to save him.

"Can I have some cereal now?"

"Sure, Cheerios?"

"Without the milk," he asks.

Already, I can see him transforming into his eccentric, creative self again.

The drive back to London is a bonding moment. His haircut is a good one that he's happy about and we stop into Chapters on the way to get him a Percy Jackson novel. He reads sixty pages in the car. We talk about confidence, and we talk about not giving up on yourself and before long, I am standing before my former wife at the truck stop.

I explain the letter and what he promised to reform in his behaviour. When he enters the car, I take it a step further.

"I would like him to live with me."

My former wife's reaction is pretended shock. She must have sensed I would go there.

"Why?"

"Because I think he needs me in his life. He needs his father now, if at the very least, for discipline's sake."

"He has two strong, male role models."

She is referring to her father and her brother. I know they love my son, but together they can't make up the bond we have. So I say it.

"He needs his father. The both of them can't take my place."

I don't mean for it to sound that aggressive, but she uses it against me anyway.

"So, your new wife becomes his mother. I still haven't forgiven you."

She blames me for making the final decision on the end of our marriage. Ten years ago now, I try my best to address the current issue.

"It's not about us. It's about him, now. I promise, I'm not trying to steal him away. I just think he can benefit from having a father every day, not to mention his brothers and sister."

"I'm sorry I haven't borne him any siblings," she says.

Now it's getting ugly and I can sense The Man in the truck nodding his head. I can almost hear what he is saying. She is not going to change her mind. You can't change her mind. She will never forgive you. People never change. She isn't a character in your book. She is a human being, born with the inability to change.

"It's not about you! It's about him. What kind of kid says he has no confidence? He needs me. We can keep the legal agreement intact, just change the residency. I'll pay for it if I have to."

This stuns her, the fact I will continue to pay her child support despite him living with me. He is in the backseat of the car and her parents are in the front seat, behind the windshield, witnessing our argument. I worry they will use the scene to turn him against me. I worry I wasted breath and my passion to save my son on the wrong battleground.

"Please, think about it."

She enters the car and I wave to my son as they speed off in the opposite direction. I listen to sad songs all the way home.

Day 11

I arrange my notes on the Governmental hospital in Bsharri, but they lack an authenticity of experience. I know the measurements of rooms, the views from others, the entire design of the ICU, where The Messenger rests, afraid to wake up to the nightmare he experienced in the bright light.

To fill in the gaps, I remember my own time in the ICU in Hamilton. Or actually, the time I spent watching the beeping monitor measure the growing blood clot in my father's brain. He fell in the garage at my uncle's house after leaving the party to go for a smoke. To this day, no one understands how it happened. My mother found him on his back, blood leaking out of his ear. I remember the scene tragically. Mid-January, minus 19 degree weather, my feet in his borrowed silk, see-through socks, freezing on the pavement as I watched my uncle pull my incoherent father up to the sitting position, his eyes rolled back before he vomited onto his lap.

The injury segregated him in a coma on the third floor of the hospital, in the ICU, for close to six months. We were told he may never wake up. What we didn't expect was the harm a feeding tube in his stomach would cause. It damaged his spinal cord and left him paralyzed from the waist down.

He did wake up, actually, the day after a nurse very rudely convinced us otherwise. It happened during my graduating year in university and it changed all of our lives. My father, the workhorse, a bull in the guise of a human being, who never once took a Tylenol, now takes a cocktail of pills every day as he tries to exist sitting down in a chair that prevents him from charging through a red flag.

I sit back on my chair in the office. It is late at night, or early morning. I can't tell. I'm struck by what I remember from those days. Countless shifts in the ICU, sleeping on hospital floors. Patrolling doctors. Visiting priests. Lost hope. Desperate prayers. Nosy relatives and friends curious to see if he had lost his mind, the one that intimidated so many with its business savvy.

I recall every detail, ingrained in my skin, tattooed to my DNA now, flowing through my veins. I recall all of the metallic scents mixed in with passing carts marked with hurried penmanship as "soiled diapers." I remember the gloomy but soft lighting in the ICU late at night, the soft green nurses' uniforms, and their white sneakers. How we fed him water with a sponge because he couldn't move to drink it from a straw, his neck inhibited by a plastic brace. How the flat-lining noise of other machines in the nearby vicinity attracted knots of green nurses and white-robed doctors. The numbers on our monitor. 84. 87. 91. Red light. Not supposed to go over 91. 91 meant more brain damage. 91 meant his brain expanding within an escapeless skull, before it caused damage the other way.

I put myself in that ICU again and combined with my research on the Bsharri hospital, I imagine The Messenger waking up, this time in the middle of the night. The softer light is wired to create a peaceful, candlelit effect. No murderous doctor is hunched over him. No complex thought process is trying to deduce the motivation of this same doctor who picked him up on the side of the road as a hitchhiker. No, The Messenger wakes in the middle of the night with a burst of delusional energy. For, when his eyes focus, his wounds stretch against their staples to shoot darts of pain across the landscape of his skin. They shoot first to his head, like a bulldozer pushing stone against the rocky ground beneath. And then they shoot to the tips of his toes, which become itchy for pain medication, or a warmer blanket.

The Messenger realizes very quickly that he is alive on the same planet, in the same human, albeit damaged form, without any benefit of escape this time. The doors are locked in the ICU. Nurses are conversing mute behind a glass window. Monitors beep, not in unison. He is thirsty. His lips are splitting apart and bleeding on the inside, onto his tongue. He coughs out loud and he imagines smoke puffing from his nose and lungs. Dusty

smoke. He doesn't know he has reached his destination, Bsharri.
He forgets his mission, temporarily. He recognizes other beds in
the vicinity, like his own, with curtains pulled back for easier
access and less privacy.

A young girl in a hospital gown walks like a death raven in
between the rows. Her skin is pale and her hair blacker than the
dark pockets with no light. She approaches his bed, dips a stick
with a tiny sponge on its end, into a yellow cup of ice water. She
squeezes it between his lips and the connection is ecstasy. He is
paralyzed by her sunken white eyes. Is she a ghost? Or another
hallucination? She disappears and he is too weak to swivel his
head. He closes his eyes and feels his tongue burning for more,
although his lips relieve themselves with the silkiness of saliva. It
has returned to his mouth.

The girl with long black hair disappears like an apparition. A
younger Madonna serving those in the rows between life and
death.

The doctor returns to take her place a short time later. It is
Sifar again, still in disguise.

"Do you believe me, now?" he says.

Sifar is intelligent with his glasses and smooth to the eye. He
is wearing a beautifully white lab coat. His green, olive skin is
exquisitely shaved as if by a sharper razor. His hands are hairless,
his fingernails tailored and manicured by a soaking in milk, it
appears.

"You did not save me?"

He whispers under the tone of the beeping monitors.

"I did save you, after I nearly killed you."

"Why would you do such a thing?"

The Messenger is uncomfortable. These few words spoken
have already dried the coolness from the sponge. His lips are
burning again.

"I create my own patients. It may be my ego."

Sifar crosses his hands delicately. They mesh together as one.
His scent is not strong or antiseptic. Just clean skin, or tree oil
natural.

"Why did you create me?"

"To play God. To play doctor. To play human. Take your pick."

"Why didn't you destroy your creation then?"

"Because I realize who you are, or rather, who you are not. Else, I might have left you to die on a cliff."

"Who am I?"

"A man dressed in borrowed clothes. Not an official. I drove away and realized something halfway to the hospital."

"What was that?"

"Humility."

"What about it?"

"It doesn't exist in that uniform. It never has. I called an ambulance right away and insisted on operating on you myself. Consider your salvation my apology."

"Who are you?"

"A man who appreciates the powerless."

"But you enjoy the power of a God."

"Which makes me appreciate the powerless that much more. Opposites attract."

"What will you do to me?"

"Set you on your way."

"What if I say anything?"

"You won't."

"How do you know that?"

"Because you are powerless, as I said. It will do no good to you and you realize this. No matter what your mind begs you to do, your body knows who it belongs to now, its debtor. It will not betray you or me."

Sifar rises from his seat on the edge of the bed, straightens his lab coat and walks away. The Messenger is appalled by the audacity of this doctor. He is also amazed by the way his body reacts when he considers exposing his crime to another. The doctor is right. His body is not his own anymore. It is indebted to its saviour.

Day 12

The Messenger convalesces to the stage of earning a private room in the step down unit. Ironic to its designation, the room is situated on a higher floor in the Bsharri hospital.

In my own, familial past, I consider the same irony when I think about my father's transfer to the step down brain injury floor in Hamilton General. Three floors above ICU, the step down floor resembled a haunted house of deranged mutant beings. Mysterious patients, securely locked in their rooms (and for good reason, mainly fear of the unknown) screamed random words in random languages, shouted out obscenities, smashed themselves into anything concrete. One man believed himself to be a sheep and he bahhhd all day and all night. Another chewed on his arm tasting it to be a chicken leg. The step down unit scared my brothers and me when we visited our father, who, like his new roommates, wasn't the same either. He didn't recognize us. He ordered my mother to make food for the invisible visitors who abided in the room with him. I never respected the power of the brain more than when I saw it broken and talking with my father's tongue. We watched it heal while he spoke words without connection, sentiments without love, while he looked at us strangely, while they tied him down because he became violent to his own body. Nothing scared us more, even when we believed he would never wake up from his coma, than the step down floor. To this day, I count my blessings he escaped the horrors within his own skull.

Unlike my father's floor of brain malfunctions, this new convalescent floor feels floating distant to The Messenger, set apart from civilization. A floor of isolation and quiet perhaps reserved for the terminally ill or those in greater need of privacy. An oasis level set above the chaos of emergency action below it. Or another level above Hell, as Dante would deem it, but one still connected to others dragging it all down into one abyss. If anything, the room resembles a tiny apartment to The Messenger instead of a medical container. The green chair in the corner appears comfortable and there is blushing colour on the walls.

The Messenger sees the same nurse periodically, or different versions of the same one, and unlike the ICU, one doesn't walk by every few minutes. He is left alone now for stretches of time. He is isolated on the island of his own bed. His only consolation is a single window with a view. He can see the milk mountains through the glass. They appear above the hospital in the upper half of the window frame. However, he hasn't gained enough strength to move on his own yet, nor developed enough neck-stretching flexibility to see what is revealed in the bottom half of the window frame. He is sure ambulances, paramedics and patients on gurneys stage the common tableau below him, at the emergency entrance—exit. At night, the red lights rise from the sign like artificial fire to make the darkening sky appear pink.

He loses track of time often, in and out of sleep, and his skin feels stretched against his ribcage, like a lace-tied corset. In the long minutes of his supine rehabilitation, he fights hard not to think of his wife, in the state of her decease (disease?), or the passing of his son; his last memory of them both on a similar bed. Another reason why he chose, multiple times, to end his life on his own terms. He considers this connection for the first time. So many failed attempts. Maybe a record somewhere in there.

He can't die like them. And he can't wait for a similar, dragged out death sentence. So he hopes.

To reassure himself everything will be all right in his end, he visualizes Kashif, his future murderer, to whom he will deliver his message. He hopes to find Kashif soon. Kashif will eliminate him expertly, as a real killer would, sparing him the guilt of trying and failing over and over again.

Having waited for his family to die in traumatic slow motion sequence inspires a craving for a specific death in The Messenger, one preferably executed in the midst of a violent act. It is a better alternative to waking up one morning only to find a new bump on your neck, or worse yet, the realization you are losing your breath in spurts of hyperventilation. The very thought of dying in his sleep disgusts The Messenger even further. After seeing his wife deteriorate on a bed into someone he couldn't recognize or fall in love with again, unlike the vibrant version he couldn't help himself from marrying, he became cynical about the value of happy endings, or peaceful endings for that matter. He believed it better to die in the midst of battle, or as a result of sacrifice, or as a victim of circumstance or accident, all of which happened suddenly and without expectation, or worse yet, waiting.

Above all else, he despises the act of waiting. To The Messenger, waiting is the real enemy. A slow torture in whatever context, waiting implies letting someone else live before you. Waiting suggests stopping when every instinct and fibre desires movement. Waiting means not living at all, really, just suspending hopes in time; a preserved death personified in the embalming of a bloodless corpse.

The Messenger seeks any distraction in his room, but the white peaks in the top frame of the window form an avalanche of snow in his imagination, rolling down the mountain, crashing through his sealed hospital window, and pummelling the heavy weight of packed snow onto his chest. What melts seeps through the recently stitched stab wounds, those in the process of healing into scars.

A collection of his wife's identities bury him in waves of white. The soft, simple way she wore her wedding dress. Her hair down, no jewelry, her great grandmother's veil with no intricate design, just pinned on flowers losing petals with every step towards the altar, with every photograph taken, some curling and browning from the popping of camera flashes or champagne bottles. And then her white hospital gown, again so simple. White cotton, one lace behind her neck like the necklace he used to help her clasp, open backed, just like her wedding gown, except this time, he could see the bulbous bones of her spinal cord protruding through a thin veneer of peeling skin.

His son's baptism gown, white again, which made him look effeminate, his long eye lashes the envy of every woman in church, his face smudged in their lipstick, holy oil blessing his forehead. White napkins, white cake, white favours, white candles, white baby shoes, white blankets, white hospital tubes, white walls, white sunlight, white Styrofoam cups, white clown faces with bloody lipstick, white moons, white stars he made to dangle from the ceiling fan in his son's room. All white, all destructive enough to kill the life he gains by waking up. So he falls asleep before it becomes dark, buried under oceans of snow. At least it is warm underneath his white sheets.

Day 13

Paris is attacked by terrorists. And bombs of unwarranted opinions explode all over Twitter and Facebook and television news channels. Previous to this shocking event, my wife reveals the results she receives from her mammogram test. There is "something there," she says. Her doctor schedules an appointment with a surgeon a week later. We have to wait. We watch the news. And talk.

"I can't believe this is happening again."

I don't know what she refers to. Does she mean the terrorist attack? Or is she alluding to another obstacle to overcome in our relationship. We've been through so many already. My painful divorce. Two virtual miscarriages. A son born with Down syndrome. All of the odds ranging in the one in a billion range.

"There is violence everywhere, even in a place like Paris."

"I suppose that is the point," she says. "Shed blood in a place of love."

"What will the surgeon do?" I ask.

"Review my tests, maybe a needle biopsy."

I don't tell her I've been researching all of the possibilities. Maybe I am testing her honesty to see if she is trying to spare me the uncertainty of her worry.

"How do you feel?"

"Scared, what else?"

I am too, but I don't know what to say, who to be. A rock, or a split branch for her to grab onto?

"We will see what he says," she assures me. She understands how sensitive I am to my own imagination. She knows me well. She knows I will think of it until every detail destroys me. I try to numb myself to the stories of those you hear almost every day. A worker's sister, the guy who used to work for my brother, the child of a girl I went to kindergarten with, only twelve years old. The Terry Fox Run scene. How my five-year-old son locked a stare on a prosthetic limb there, thinking it a trick or a funny bone pulled expertly out of an electrified hole in The Operation Game. Like me, he doesn't sleep well when he becomes sensitive to a fear.

Since that walk, he asks questions unbecoming of a five-year-old boy, or rather, becoming his ignorance.

"You won't die," he asks his mother before she tucks him into bed after a requested cuddle. He doesn't know a thing, but the fear speaks for itself. It also speaks for me. We love her the same, I think to myself, or fear the loss of her in our lives, the same way. I feel like one of her children and maybe this is the excuse for our similar panic. Losing the mother in her we so desperately need as men afraid of every threatening domestic detail we are not designed to accomplish with the same grace.

The Man from my walk-in closet sits between my wife and me on the couch as we watch the stories from the terrorist attack. Two gunmen enter a Parisian café and start shooting. As random as a video game, as horrifying as one of his off-the-wall ideas. Another bomb-clad individual tries to enter the soccer stadium only to be refused by a security guard, who pushes him far enough not to hurt anyone else but himself. The invasion by random gunman of a heavy metal concert in a theatre. Again, what seems like an unfamiliar event in the city of love. Open fire on an audience facing the stage. Suspension of disbelief destroyed by an unsuspecting bullet in the back.

The reported, contextual details are eerily similar. Smoke. Shattered glass. Red lights and wandering bystanders left bleeding as they sit on the curb in the embrace of a stranger in uniform.

My wife is frozen. I try to feel sorry for those who passed away so suddenly, but like The Messenger, I am comparing deaths. I can't help myself. It is morbid thinking, or so The Man tries to mediate the space between us. My wife disappears for a moment to start the air popper in the kitchen.

"What are you doing?"

"What do you mean, what am I doing?"

"She needs to hear reassurance and all you can think about is that stupid messenger of yours. Who do you feel more sorry for? He is alive, for God's sake. You spared him. But you can't spare her, only a doctor can do that. You are powerless, like your doctor/murderer said when he gloated to The Messenger."

"Whatever I say will explode between us, perhaps killing you too," I say.

"You are selfish," he says.

He is right, to so many degrees. It is hard to admit how much you depend upon someone to fulfill your life. How she fills in the spaces while life happens, so that life can happen.

"I don't know what to say, right now. Everything is suspended. We are waiting."

"She is suffering, while you wait."

I never assumed The Man carried any sensitivity. I stereotyped him, I suppose, not realizing that, as his creator, I could do such a thing.

"Killers have hearts too, you know," he says.

"You care about my wife?"

I am still skeptical as I have always seen him as someone who is beyond the weakness of care. The Man, or in my design of him, is immune to the circumstances that make us human. Like an insane man, or my father in the step down unit, or Kashif, whom my reader is about to meet for the first time in this book. The Man is a self-emptying shell that is always looking for a temporary fill, not realizing he leaks from the inside out.

"That is harsh. Is that what you really think of me?"

Once again, I am annoyed by his skill of reading my mind.

"Are you ready to re-enter the story?" I ask him. I am trying to change the subject. I can hear my wife shuffling popcorn into a separate bowl.

"I never liked Lebanon. I will find my way back into the story, in due time."

"No, you won't. I will write you in when I see fit," I promise him, disguising a threat.

"As you say, master, writer."

He laughs to himself a little when my wife returns. The news is almost all red now. Reports appear with the Eiffel Tower in the background. They are geographically situating terrorism, promoting their stories against the appropriate backdrop. It is theatre and the stage is reset by the world's association with Paris again, except this time there are no lights. Only red, emergency lights and blankets sprawled over dead bodies on the street.

"How can you stop this from happening?" I ask my wife. She is folding laundry now. She removed her contacts and is wearing her glasses.

"Some things happen for no apparent reason but to be," she stops herself.

Another news reporter interrupts our fragmented conversation. The Man has disappeared. I think I see him on the television screen, walking by a crime scene. I blink my eyes and when I do so, I don't see him anymore. I am hallucinating. Invisible stress is occupying me, I consider. I need to see a doctor but I don't want to suggest it to my wife. I believe this could be a trigger for the argument we haven't had. That even in her potential life threatening sickness, I need the help of an outside source to straighten my mind out.

"Do you remember Cape Cod?" I ask her.

The thought of it brings an automatic smile to her face.

"I miss Cape Cod. Remember the day we arrived. We were early and they wouldn't let us into the room, so we stripped down and jumped into the ocean because the waves were high."

"Yeah, it was so much fun."

"I have never had so much fun, in all of my life."

"You wore that white bikini."

"You liked that white bikini."

"I loved it. I loved that time. I love you," I say to her.

She stares at me and then stops folding the laundry.

I can feel her tears seeping through my shirt and to my shoulder when I have her in my arms.

DAY 14

The pressure of my wife's test results and the possibility of cancer make us more intimate. Our kisses are softer. Our lovemaking is more sensory and frequent. We reserve our nights to fall asleep together, combining our body heat to thaw the coldness of the next day's reality. We fight against this reality in the morning by exploring the intimacy of our warm skin and softer touches. I am a lucky man, I often think in those early mornings. I sleep next to a woman who is as beautiful to the touch as she is to the imagination. In the darkness of the early morning we find the opportunity to whisper our attraction to one another. We rush sex and sneak around so the kids don't hear or wake. We do so understanding we have not outgrown each other, that our first passion remains, despite what we've been through, or are about to go through.

I adore the way she falls on me in these moments, how our bodies understand the timing of our desires with no language, only movement and sensory appreciation. I find her easily in the dark and it assures me I can do the same during the day, or in the light of tragic news.

Our kids infiltrate the scene with the worst sense of timing and we often regret our hiding and sneaking around under the covers, where we pretend to sleep, where it becomes a game to keep us covered until we are decent enough not to traumatize our children with the naked bodies of their parents.

"We are horrible parents," she giggles under the sheets while they beg to join us on the bed, while I try to find my underwear near the foot of the bed, rolled up in between sheets.

"We always find a way," I joke.

She reads into it a little more than I expected and jumps on me to kiss me violently.

Our kids are not impressed and one of them starts crying.

"Are we ready to eat?" I announce.

This pacifies their disapproval of our physical intimacy.

When I make it to school that morning, I am energized and happy. I feel confident my wife will defeat this scare and we will find a way to keep making love around it.

And then I throw a book at a student and my world is turned upside down again.

I don't know what came over me. I walk into school in the early morning like a sexually redeemed husband in a Cialis commercial. My first class, with my locally developed kids, goes well. They understand the novel I am teaching them and are surprising me with their insights. And then second period comes around. My senior Writer's Craft class. As I await them filing in, I can hear some giggling about not having their assignment in for the class. Others complain about a printer not working in the library downstairs. When I have them settled, I can see that only a few have their assignment ready on their desks. It is a creative writing class and this term, I have an eclectic bunch, to say the least. I am disappointed in their failed effort. It is nearing Christmas and I detect their attention declining. Even as I am trying to get them to settle down, they are speaking under my voice. So my introduction to the day's lesson transforms into a state of the union address. I offer these on occasion to my students. One usually comes before Christmas break, the other during Spring Fever. It simply reminds them of important deadlines and evaluations left over. It almost always follows the theme of picking up the intensity instead of sitting on your current mark.

I am in the midst of this state of the union and I can hear my voice rising. I rarely, if ever, raise my voice. I feel I am lucky my students respect me as a teacher and writer, and in this class, this respect is only magnified by inspired moments of creative ideas and mentoring. However, on this day, there is a new sharpness to my voice. I can feel it cutting the air. Everyone in the class is attentive to the alacrity of every word.

Worse yet, I can hear the echo of my voice, so it must be loud. As I reach a climax in my lecture, about how sacred an act it is to create something on paper, and how reflective it is of everything they find important in their young lives, one of the students in the second row takes out her cellphone. She is texting and doing absolutely nothing to disguise it.

"Are you serious!" I lower my voice an octave but raise it a few decibels higher. She pretends not to hear me. She thinks it is directed to the rest of the class in general.

I grab an edition of Macbeth (we are studying it in my grade 11 class) and aim for the exposed phone. The pages feather up, change the direction of the toss, and swipe her on the arm. She is scared. I can tell from her reaction she is scared, as are those around her. They didn't expect me to throw something. I didn't expect me to throw something. I think about it for a split second before realizing that I actually threw something. My voice is functioning without me.

"Are you serious!" I repeat. "You are texting someone right now!"

With no other option but to follow through, I grab my water bottle next and throw it into the recycling bin. A few of the students flinch. They have never seen me angry and I can tell they simply want it to end. Not to overdo the drama, I assign them a shitload of seatwork and the class is quiet and studious. However, the girl is shaky. She is still scared.

After about five minutes she leaves the room without asking.

I wait. I walk out of the room to see if she is crying in the hallway at the same time suspecting where she has gone.

I get a call from the vice principal ten minutes later.

"I have a girl from your class here, she is crying."

"Do you want me to come down?"

"Yes. I'll send another teacher up."

I find her in the office with the other vice principal.

Amelia is crying and shaking in the chair and I can't help myself from feeling sorry for her. She is a student who understands my sense of humour, but is completely shocked by my sense of anger. She doesn't throw me under the bus, though. All she wants is to go home.

Our other vice principal is a lady I worked with at another school. She is bluntly honest with an erected tough exterior, but softhearted. She encourages Amelia to stay in school.

"Going home will only draw more attention to it the next day. I'm sure it wasn't intentional," she says, and then she looks at me to continue her train of thought.

"It wasn't, and I'm sorry."

Just as I apologize, I feel The Man entering the room uninvited. He is speaking to me in between the awkward spaces of trying to convince this girl to stay at school.

"What has happened to you? She will throw you under the bus in a flash. Don't feel sorry for her. She is dramatizing the whole event. Can't you see she is desiring your attention?"

I try to ignore him. I am worried I have seriously scarred this girl.

"Your pathetic inclination to pity is making your story boring. It's your tragic flaw as a writer and the reason you haven't published more. You feel sorry for yourself. You feel sorry for your characters. It's not your job to pity your characters. It's the reader's job to do that. You have to create them as empathetic. You love them too much, you like your students too much, or else The Messenger would have already met Kashif. Instead, you have him toiling in a hospital room thinking about his wife, feeling sorry for himself. It's tragically contagious, if you ask me."

The girl keeps using the same tissue to dry her tears, so I offer her another one.

"Listen, we can get over this. Let me walk you back to class. I promise, it won't ever happen again."

"What is she, your wife now?" The Man laughs out loud. "You can't show weakness to a student, just like you can't show weakness to the characters you create. They will take advantage of you."

I must be listening to The Man too much because the vice principal is repeating a question in my direction.

"Are you all right? Can you walk her back to class now?"

Apparently, my student has agreed to the idea of sticking around. It is an awkward walk back to class. I remind her how much I appreciate our previous rapport. How I would rather make her laugh than cry. We stop at the foot of the stairway and I tell her I get too passionate about writing while explaining how I want her to be serious about her own talents. How disturbing it was to see she cared more about the person she was texting.

"Are we all right?" I ask.

She nods.

The rest of my students watch as she takes her seat. I try to joke it off to let them know all is resolved, but I am worried I have hurt her in some way.

When I return home from work, my wife is waiting with our daughter at the bus stop. I tell her what happened from the car window, while my daughter tries to hitch a ride in the truck.

"It's okay," my wife says. I expect her to say we don't need this right now, but she doesn't.

"She should have known not to bring her cell phone to class."

"I know. I still feel bad about it."

"I bet she is over it. You have to get over it," she recommends.

Perhaps, like The Man, she knows me too well. I harp on things, especially when it is me making the mistake. I recall it a million times, with all of the details, and every time I think about it, I do more damage to the regret. The Man is right, I feel sorry myself. Perhaps, like my Messenger, I ask for bad luck, or invite it subconsciously.

After the chaos of feeding the clan, getting them bathed and in bed, I return to the computer. I creep on Twitter and Facebook to see if my tirade made the gossip news. I don't see any evidence of it. Perhaps, as my wife suggested, it was nothing. Or perhaps it is only something to me.

At night, I decide it is time to empower The Messenger. He is healing nicely and as humans are prone to do, he feels more alive mentally, even sexually.

So I revisit him in his hospital room. And I introduce something unfamiliar to him since his wife passed—a sexual fantasy. When he pulled off the road and carried the tiger to the hidden habitation in the woods, I did have him leave at night because he was worried of an attraction he felt towards the boy's mother.

It scared him to think he could be attracted to anyone but his wife, despite thoughts of it when he was married to her, when he was away at his job halfway across the world. From a distance, the loneliness inspired thoughts of adultery and this is one of the reasons why he wants to die in the present. He thinks he deserves it. He thinks having those thoughts actually created the punishment of his family's death. That they are one in the same. Cause and effect.

The nurse who now bathes him in his room with a sponge resurrects the sexual instinct in him. He worked with many attractive women at the U.N. Strong, intellectual, sexualized women with high levels of testosterone. Aggressive women who could keep secrets, who wanted to live adventurous lives, who considered time zones justification for sexual experimentation.

There was one media officer in particular. Her name was Cheryl. Straight blonde hair cut sharply at the ends to reveal a portion of her long neck. A properly posed smile. Her eyes smiled at him as well, as did her body language in his presence. She leaned on him, shoulder to shoulder, placed her hand on his forearm to get his attention. She was never overly flirtatious or bubbly, but he felt an inner pull around her. He considered acting on it at times. He imagined the moment their mutual physical interests would cross. He didn't know a single thing about her, other than her job title and name. She made him feel good about himself, perhaps even younger, or more nostalgic for those younger, simpler days.

One night, on a peace conference in Cambodia, she wished him good night in a darkened hallway. He could hear the ice machine around the corner sending water through an osmosis system, and then stop. It became quiet. She wore her glasses that evening and his search for her face behind them invigorated that pull. She spoke in a sonnet's sequence. Each line designed to rhyme with another down the road.

"Do you ever wonder what we are searching for?" she asked with one foot holding the door of her hotel room open.

"Violence and peace," he answered. In retrospect, he felt stupid for trying so hard to impress her.

"We go from place to place and stick our noses in someone else's history. Always in places where we don't belong. We are like the worst kinds of tourists."

"I know. It is condescending, isn't it?"

"That's it exactly. That we should investigate their cultures, or assume we have the right to judge them on a scale that balances the benefits of war and peace."

She removed her glasses and he interpreted the gesture as an invitation. He wanted to move closer to her. He wanted to breach the crest of the wave about to smash into a sandy shoreline and dissolve into it, but he stopped himself. He remembered every detail of that moment. The musty fog of air and mosquitos in the hallway. The hum of the ice machine, the falling crash of water congealing into ice in the darkness of a cooling bin. The length of her body leaning into the door frame. Half of it inside her room already, the other keeping the conversation going. They had never spoken about their opinions. He had often thought about his career path, his service to peacemaking. But he had never discussed the hypocrisy of it with someone else. She rested her face on the door frame now, like it could help her close her eyes and fall asleep.

"I suppose we are middle people," he said. "We stand in the middle and try to see both sides of the conflict. And then we invite others to join us in no man's land only to realize it is more dangerous than taking sides."

She nodded and sighed a little. Her agreement lit up the sensory mechanisms on his chest. He could feel air exhaling from all of his pores now, his nervous stomach pumping the circulation of the flow.

"Good night."

She paused to stare at him one last, awkward time. Her wedding ring sparkled on the door frame. She tapped it against the door when he didn't respond. She was waiting for him to make the next step, to take sides, to leave the middle of his doubt to venture onto her side, which didn't appear so dark in real life as it did in the context of his seedling guilt.

"Good night," he returned under his breath. He wondered if she had heard him because she paused again, frozen.

He turned his back and that Christmas, when he returned home, the diagnosis of his wife's illness confirmed the sin in his heart.

This time around, in the Bsharri hospital, the very thought of sin or guilt never crosses The Messenger's mind.

The nurse with long black hair carefully removes the hospital gown covering the scarring stab wounds. When she does so, his skin tingles. Her fingerprints are soft and gentle, her skin silky on the drying areas of his. He stares at her while she pulls the gown down and away from his body. When she leans over the bed to pull the part of the sheet stuck in the hospital bed bars, her breasts press into his belly. She works away oblivious to how he sees her. Frustrated with a resistant sheet, she walks over to the other side and he can see her panty line beneath the green scrub pants. These details make him nervously hungry, as he felt that night in Cambodia. He tries hard to dismiss the way his body is reacting to her presence. She doesn't speak to him. She simply moves to prepare. To prepare her work assignment in the most efficient manner possible. She doesn't recognize how these movements inspire a fleet of cold pimples down his body. Even his feet feel funny now, tingly as well, heated.

She rolls up her sleeves and prepares the sponge. She doesn't rush, as he expects her to. And she is not ruthless with the work. She begins with his hair. She presses it back with the wet sponge, in even strokes, so that it doesn't get too wet, so that it doesn't drip onto his pillow. To ensure this, she tucks one towel under his neck by pulling him into her chest. He smells her skin and sees constellations of tiny little moles and freckles darkened by sun.

When she returns him gently to the towel covering his pillow, he smiles at her. She smiles back and nods. She then proceeds to place towels under his entire body. She lines up rolls on one side but not before helping him to lay in the fetal position. She unravels the towels and returns him to his back. She does the same on the other side but this time leaves him in the fetal position.

She bathes him with a cloth and sponge, like a mother would gently to a newborn. With his back turned to her, he tries hard to settle the shiver of his body. He isn't cold. If anything, he is overheating, the wetness of his hair posing as a perspiring forehead.

Her touch arouses him and for every ounce of shame and decency, he can't stop his body from reacting. When she turns him over, flat on his back, he has grown noticeably to her. She doesn't react. Perhaps she has seen this overreaction to the sponge bath before. She continues without skipping a beat, as if not to notice. She blesses his feet with the warmth of a wet towel, while he closes his eyes to pretend sleep. This may spare him some shame, he believes.

Until she touches it.

He opens his eyes and she is stroking it softly with her finger pressed on the inside of the sponge. She catches him watching her but shows no reaction to his embarrassment. His face feels like it is reddened with rash while she continues to stroke it gently with the sponge. In her eyes, he imagines what she is thinking. That he is perverted, or starved for a woman's touch. Or maybe she believes him to be a man with no self-control.

She stops suddenly to place the dried out sponge on his belly. He feels completely exposed to her now, his body, his thoughts, his imagination, his desires—all vulnerable to her simple touch. He expects her to dry his pulsating skin with a towel but she doesn't yet.

Instead, she places her hand around it and strokes it further until he releases himself into her hand with a repressed moan.

She wipes his belly with the sponge again and lets his skin air dry as she collects her cleaning supplies.

He says thank you under his breath. She leaves the room not hearing it as an invitation to stay.

Day 15

The Messenger finds a surrogate home in the Bsharri hospital. His discharge is delayed, according to the nurse he is sexually attracted to. Her nametag reads Sahal and she is surprised to find he also speaks her language, which is sign. She doesn't voice words. He is unsure if it is a physical disability or a mental one. Whether she is not able to speak, or whether she chooses to be mute. On his end, he enjoys the silence between them. How she communicates to him with the touch of her hand. He never once considered his body this landscape of mysteries until she touched it. In the mirror, it had always appeared as one embedded with land mines and irreparable failure marks. But there are other meanings she unearths in her explorations of it, buried truths.

He discovered her inability to speak after another intimate bathing session. Once again, her very presence in the room inspired a physical compulsion in him. And for a second time, she appeased it with a skin-to-skin touch, after which he desired to talk to her. He wanted to express his sexual attraction to her outright and apologize for it. He worried if her interpretation of his arousal demeaned her in any way. He also craved reassurance from her. Despite his automatic attraction to her presence in the room, he didn't expect her to relieve him of this internal torture every time she entered to care for him. She didn't respond to his questions or apologies. She nodded and smiled. Smiled and nodded. After the first time, he understood the embarrassment of not having anything to say. Now that she had crossed the line twice, he needed to know how she felt about it. For some reason, he required a guarantee she did this to him only. Like an awkward commitment or promise ring of sorts.

After he spoke to her, she didn't respond by voice. He tried to get her attention while she collected her bathing materials, but to no avail. She didn't flinch at the sound of his voice.

So he waited for her to catch his eyes before he tried sign language.

His message made her blush red.

"Thank you for reminding me I am alive," he had said with his hands.

She responded in kind.

"You have many scars."

"I have fought many battles," he answered, "more with myself."

She nodded. She understood.

She then walked over to the head of his bed. He observed the roundness of her breasts, the soft skin between her chin and neck. She extended her arm before his eyes and he saw scarred lines there at the wrists.

He expected her to cry. The very coincidence of their mutual attempts to die almost persuaded him to do so himself.

"I want you to stay. When you leave, I wait for you to come back," he gestured before rambling with his hands.

"When you come back, I never want you to go. When you go, I think about you until you return."

She placed a hand over her mouth to prevent an obscene burst of laughter, or a grunt.

The quiet in their exchanges combined with the effort to communicate with her in sign created a poem between them. Sign language. His interpretation of her sign language and the secrets beneath the surface of her own skin. How they motivated those same fingers which squeezed him ever so gently and firmly to make him release himself into her hands.

Abruptly, she turned as if to hear something in the dead quiet of the floor. She walked over to the door and locked it again as if to imply she needed privacy to bathe her patient. Except this time, she removed her white nurse's shoes, climbed over the steel railing at the foot of the bed and sat crosslegged there.

She removed her top and unclasped her bra. Her breasts fell and peaked at their darkened nipples. She placed both hands on each of his legs. He trembled in their tightening grip on his skin.

This time, she placed him in her mouth and swallowed him.

The Man interrupts this sequence with sarcasm.

"So you are writing pornography now?" he jabs.

My office is quiet and the lighting is soft at three in the morning. I waited for my wife to fall into a deep sleep before I escaped down here. Or else, she might have thought our recent love-making renaissance cheapened by the departure of her husband to another passion.

"Just because you are getting more of it these days, doesn't mean it has to spill into the story. You were about to introduce him to the protagonist? And you had to write another sexual scene before that? To what purpose, it baffles me."

He sits on the leather sofa, below my degrees. His words reveal jealousy tonight, as if he feels cheated himself not to have slept with this woman first.

"Of course I am. Who wouldn't be jealous of a relationship with no talking and the only means of communication sexual?"

I laugh at his sarcasm and he smirks at me. Sex scenes are very difficult to write and I know he understands the challenge. He is simply growing impatient with the plot of the story.

"You need to get him out of that room now. It is becoming a haven. The sex is fine and I really like Sabal."

He hums to himself as if to imagine.

"But our protagonist is literally around the corner, a few rooms down, so you have the opportunity to kill two birds with one storyline. Have them meet in body at the hospital. How will you do so without making it appear contrived? Now that you've given The Messenger a girlfriend, he will be hard-pressed to find the man who he knows will murder him. This will stall the story, improve his character development, mind you, but practically force you to come up with a miracle to introduce Kashif."

The Man is right. I know creating a transition between the act of love and the act of death is a difficult one. He is correct to fear the wonky bridge between the two. The Messenger, after his sexual gravitation to Sabal, will be inclined to stall his meeting with Kashif. What The Man and The Messenger don't realize is that character is not the only driving force behind story. The Messenger is guiding the point of view, yes. However, a story is happening below the surface right next door in the hospital. There, in a similar hospital room, rests the motivation behind every one of Kashif's present and future actions. His daughter, delicately dying.

So I have Sabal convince The Messenger to stand up one day. He does so on weaker knees. Before long, he is walking strong enough to venture outside their secret love nest. She proudly shows him off to other nurses in the hallway. They smile at him, some suspiciously, like they know.

As The Messenger walks the parade route to the well-lit waiting room at the end of the hall he glances into the neighbouring rooms. He is curious to know if others abide with him on this step down floor. Or did he receive special privileges from the doctor who attempted to murder him before saving him for one more chance at accomplishing his mission.

When he glances into one of the rooms, he sees a golden haired man with an angular jaw. The man is standing directly centered in the doorway with his arms crossed. The Messenger sees a pair of white, narrow feet at the edge of the hospital bed. The feet are delicate and feminine enough to hint at the salvation of a glass slipper.

The golden haired man stares back for an instant before The Messenger shifts his attention to the next room.

He doesn't know what he expects to see. He doesn't even know what he wants to see. His curious, former self must be creeping up on him again, he fears. In his private room, his only focus is Sabal and her visits. In the hallway, he feels eyes observing him, some of them blue and evil.

Sabal has two hospital trays facing one another in the emptied waiting room. Her smile is wider and prouder.

She points to the dishes. They don't resemble the measured portions. And there is no intrinsic metallic or plastic smell to the aroma of the food. He realizes at once this is a homemade meal. She had made him lunch.

"From my garden," she gestures.

The tomatoes in the salad are blood red paste tomatoes and the softer, goat cheese is ghost white.

"From my heart," she gestures again.

He notices a slab of reddened meat dripping watery blood into the other contents.

She approaches him closely, her breasts pressing into his bony chest, her hips magnetized to his. She slips her hand down to cup him.

He understands very quickly without her gesturing what she means by the inclusion of real meat in his diet.

The Messenger basks in the bright sun on his back as he eats the homemade meal. Sabal doesn't eat much. She is watching him eat and enjoying the food more this way. In her blackened eyes, he sees so much relativity, so much inherent understanding, like the actualization of a past life rediscovered. That's how he feels and can't express in sign language. Like they already know each other before the invention of words.

In the doorway, the man with golden hair walks by. He eerily surveys the scene from the corner of his lighter eyes. He walks away.

"Who is that?" The Messenger asks when Sabal also notices.

"I don't know. A new visitor. Never saw him before."

After they finish lunch, The Messenger feels dizzy at first. He has not eaten this amount of food for quite some time. By the time they return to the room, the blood in the red meat kicks in. He closes the door in behind him, embraces Sabal from behind and then pushes her onto the bed, her face down in his slept-in sheets.

He then rips her pants down and returns the oral stimulation from behind. She doesn't moan or make a sound. He could feel her trembling on his tongue, dripping onto it.

She pulls him by the hair up and punches him hard on the side. He doesn't understand this message. She keeps assigning it to him with force, the punches stronger and faster. He looks over to her face. She is biting the sheets now, no sound, no growl. He can hear a rip in the sheet.

He forces himself into her and she snaps her head back. Now she is slapping the mattress. Something is bothering her, disrupting his rhythm. She swings her arms back and they flail into him. Some of the blows nearly wind him. She is insistent and violent in these gestures as he increases his speed. He is breathing heavy and feeling faint again.

Finally, she stops and removes him cold. He is suspended before she leads him to the spot she wants him to re-enter. He nearly hyperventilates but does as he is told and she returns again to biting his bed.

It hurts and there is blood on him now. When he releases himself in her, her neck twists and her face is sinister, almost out of body.

Day 16

For the next three days, The Messenger searches for Sabal on the hospital floor. She has disappeared or has been reassigned. He takes regular walks now on his own. There is strength in his legs and his feet harden more with every step.

On each of these walks, he notices a different visitor in the neighbouring room. First, it was the golden haired man. The next day, it is a tall, brunette woman. On the third day, another tall woman dressed in a full niqab and hijab. Her neck snaps when she sees him in the hallway. He worries his naked legs have insulted her.

The Messenger grows more curious about the neighbouring patient. He wants to enter her room and see more of her than her pale white feet at the end of the bed. Every time he sees the door open, another visitor is in the place of the last. Staring at her. Praying over her. As silent as his communication is with Sabal.

On the fourth day, The Messenger asks the nurse on the floor if Sabal is scheduled to visit him for a sponge bath.

The nurse, with curly black hair and dramatic red lipstick nods no, before shuffling paper into a folder.

"Has she been transferred elsewhere?" The Messenger interrupts her work again.

"No, no, no. She works every floor."

"Will she return to this floor?"

The nurse at the desk stops her diligence to whisper over the counter.

"Do you think you are the only one?"

The Messenger is too taken aback to answer. He previously assumed he had chased Sabal away after their last sexual interlude. He worried he might have crossed a line.

"Am I not the only one?"

The nurse returns to her paperwork and The Messenger walks to the waiting room. It is not as bright in mid-afternoon as it is in the morning. From the platform of this room, which juts out separately from the building, the surrounding mountains are shadowed white, like eggshells in an overcast sky. He remembers his mission, before returning his focus to Sabal.

He recalls the words of the nurse again and he is humiliated by his belief in them. He needs to find Sabal, so he descends the stairs to other hallways. When he can't find her, he takes flights with ease and anger, surprising himself with his newfound strength. He reaches a hallway and hears a conglomeration of nurses laughing in a tiny room behind the counter. He can smell the heated fabric of their combined lunches and he gags a little in his mouth.

They talk loudly in a native dialect.

"She calls herself the cure. The audacity."

An uproar of laughter and hands slapping a hard surface.

"She spreads more disease than she cures, that's for sure."

The energy rising, with voices contagious.

"I believe she can talk and hear everything. It is the only way she keeps her job."

The Messenger feels a chill rise from the floor to spread like a vine on his back. He descends the stairs to his floor. When he passes his neighbour's room, the patient is finally alone. He sneaks into it. A girl lies on her back on a bed of black hair. It spreads like an oil spill on a white sheet. She wears glasses and her skin is cream white. Her eyes are closed. She appears dead but for the breathing mechanism slithering up the side of her nose. She appears asleep but for the heart beat number on the screen. The room is tranquil, exquisitely clean. No flowers from her visitors. No cards. No soft, pastel personalized gifts. No signs that she belongs to anyone but the room. The Messenger stands in the spot of her visitors. It is no wonder they don't approach her. There is a glow about the space surrounding her bed, like hallowed ground before a burning bush. Stepping near it may disrupt the sacred vigil. The girl reminds The Messenger of the saint in the grotto, deceased, entombed in a see-through glass coffin for the world to observe the miracle of resisting decomposition.

In the late still night, Sabal enters his room and wakes him. Her face is not the same. She is another woman without the vulnerability of his nakedness, without sunlight in the room. She is not dressed in her hospital garments. She is wearing a jacket and scarf and her face emanates a cool breeze.

Is he dreaming her?

He turns over in the bed to release his hands enough to speak. He stops himself.

"You can hear me. You can speak to me."

"Yes, I can."

"Why do you lie to me?"

"To strengthen you, my dear. You were weak and defeated. Now you are strong and angry."

"Why do you do these things to me? Why?" The Messenger stops himself remembering how he initiated the connection, how his body invited her to engage.

She places her hand on his chest. Her hands are fire and her face is ice. She has come in from the outside, from the cold. She has snuck into his room. She is going away? She is in no rush to leave.

"It is time for you to escape."

"You want me to leave with you?"

"No, I want you to leave without me. You are strong now. If you stay any longer, you will weaken again. I know you have a mission."

"What mission?"

She searches for someone else in the room who doesn't exist to lend credibility to her instruction.

"You will not find who you are looking for unless you leave. You need to leave now before anyone else sees you."

"Who told you about my mission?"

"A man, a very horrible man."

I stop writing. And then I start looking for him. The Man. Nowhere in my research notes did I intend to reintroduce him at this stage in the story as a mysterious character. As I often do when I am writing in a zone, I try my best to write instinctively, subconsciously. To me, this is the most sincere part of the process. Listening to my characters or letting the story come to me instead of imposing upon it with an outline. The Man must have seen this opening to intrude himself upon the story. I realize he is outsmarting me. He has found a way to access the story outside my ability to create it with words. I sensed his attraction to Sabal and I realize how invested he is in the story. How did he manage to reach Sabal without me writing it down first? With only one way of knowing, I resume my writing. A character always manages to reveal motivation at some point or another so perhaps I can find it in between the lines or better yet, find him in between my lines.

"What did this man sound like, Sabal?" The Messenger insists.

"Very calm. He came to me in my sleep. I felt him inside of me as real."

"Did he take you?"

"Yes, I dreamt of him. At first I felt him as I did you, the night before. Then I realized the man behind me, the man inside of me, was someone else. His voice frightens me."

"Why did you lie to me?"

"Because words scare me. Soft words, love words, words that know me. All of them scare me. I can trust actions. I can trust eyes. I can trust scent and skin. I can never trust words. When I saw you could speak with your hands, I realized I could have a real friend."

"Then why do you whore yourself to the hospital?"

"Because I am a whore by nature. I came here as a whore, left for dead by a group of men who recognized me as such. I healed as a whore. I was given a job because I am a whore. I can't change who I am. Only words can change me and I've given up on them. I don't want to change. I want to sink into myself, lose who I am in silence and feel pleasure like a whore."

"What did he say to you, this man?"

"He said to leave you alone. To not see you or else he would silence me for good."

"Does he know you are here?"

"I don't know. You have to leave."

"Are you leaving?"

"I will not be the same after I leave this room. Remember me as I am now."

Sabal kisses him softly on the cheek and runs out of the room. When The Messenger follows her into the hallway, she is darker than the vacuous air swallowing the red emergency exit lights. It is late at night and the nurse on duty is absent or asleep at the table where she eats her nighttime lunch. The Messenger sees that the door is open in the next room. The man standing in the space before the bed has blackened skin. His eyeballs are very white. He walks over to The Messenger.

"Come with me."

The man's face is deeper black upon approach and oily. His eyeballs are bone white. He is wearing the garment of a priest, with a bleached collar.

"Where?"

"To the place where you will tell me your message."

The Messenger is stronger now. He finds it difficult to understand why he is empowered, even after hearing that Sabal cheated him in some way. Is it the fulfilment of his mission or is it Sabal's betrayal and escape from his fated life?

"Is there a cliff where you live?" The Messenger asks.

"Yes."

"Then I will follow you there."

The Messenger never imagined finding the black priest in his neighbour's room. He follows him towards the Exit sign at the end of the hallway and wonders how far Sabal has gone from the hospital.

Day 17

The Man, like Sabal in the story, mysteriously disappears from my life. He doesn't visit me while I shore up my research for the second half of the novel and he doesn't interrupt my daily routine to remind me not to take too much time away from the novel. Momentum is very important in the first draft of a novel. One day's work seeps into the next day's appetite to create. When I completed my M.A. in English literature and Creative Writing, my poet professor once said that the most difficult aspect of writing is self-discipline and motivation. Similarly, Stephen King notes in his memoir that it is better to write the entire first draft from day to day, to its very end, or else you may disrupt the energy that compels you to write in the first place.

I suppose it is a matter of suspension of disbelief. In order for a reader to want to continue reading he or she must suspend disbelief that the story is fictional. In turn, while the writer is writing, he or she must also suspend disbelief that the story is worth writing.

Although I expect The Man to reappear when I least suspect or want him to, I appreciate the time to relearn what I previously researched for the story. I find some fascinating material, which may or may not find itself in this novel. Like the Al-Qaeda note-books unearthed after the invasion of Iraq in 2003. They detail and depict with drawings various torture techniques used to extract information from foreign captives. From using a hot flat iron to tying a prisoner to chains attached to a truck, to stretching arms backwards over a door, the journals themselves present a history of resistance from the other side not documented by biased CNN reports on terrorism, or hidden C.I.A. files on pris-oner treatment in Guantanamo Bay.

The specifics of the research invigorate me, I suppose. But in this case, my fascination with the darker details is much more involved. These forbidden details, often flagged by librarians or federal agents scavenging email correspondences or social media threats, are opening up hidden avenues to empathize with my protagonist.

How could I possibly empathize with him, I often doubt. My protagonist is a terrorist, through and through. The terror he has created from killing innocent victims in the course of their daily lives is atrocious in nature. Children, unsuspecting bystanders, tourists, and even loyal animals have perished due to his interpretation of a greater cause. He is despicable from the perspective of his history, or rather, his fingerprints upon it. And yet, I feel for him. And it's not because his daughter is dying slowly for his sins in the same hospital from which The Messenger has recently discharged himself. No, no, no. If anything, there may be some critics who will consider this motivation slightly cliché in nature, although I do have some twists in store.

So why is Kashif, my numb, unfeeling protagonist, worthy of my sympathy? Perhaps The Man was right. Maybe I feel sorry for my characters because their creator feels sorry for himself. Is it possible to inherit this trait, albeit genetically, from creator to creation? Adam didn't inherit his ability to create from God, although he was created in his likeness? Instead, he was assigned the responsibility of naming his creator's creations? Is this employment god-like? Was this construct doomed to fail from the start with a little taste of the forbidden fruit?

I think deeply about my protagonist. By this point, I consider him something more than a friend, someone less real than family due to our inseparable differences. I could never imagine killing to prove a point or obliterating innocence to make it memorable. And yet, I kill off my characters solely to speed up the pace of a plot. Or worse yet, I kill them with the hidden agenda of making them memorable after the story is over. To make them immortal, I suppose.

So how am I any different than Kashif. He kills real people and I kill fictional people for a living. That's one major difference. He kills for a belief, I kill for entertainment, which makes me sound much worse. He is willing to sacrifice anything to create story and I am on the fence. Does it mean that much to me, creating story? Am I prepared to go to the ultimate end to see it through, for blood to have more blood, as Macbeth put it?

The Man finds me in the midst of this deliberation as I tidy up the English storage room at school. I am alone, after school, and it is quiet. Due to the size and waste of space in the English storage room, I previously asked our principal if it would be okay to create a quiet, lounge-like marking area. Of course she completely disagreed and rejected the idea. So instead, I clear a spot in the room because I have decided to sacrifice my lunch on a daily basis in order to write some more. Usually, I write late at night but the story is calling me strong during the day so I need to at least use my lunch time to read over the previous day's work. In doing so, I get a head start at night, not to mention the use of my brain in the course of the day and not at its suffocating end.

"You should be home and you know it. Your wife is receiving her test results today."

I laugh to myself. Although The Man doesn't know it, I purposely stalled the story with some philosophical renderings in order to smoke him out of his hole. The Man thinks he is the only one who can infiltrate. He has been avoiding me since he ambushed the story and one of my characters, Sabal, in between the lines, or in between page breaks. I am also aware how such an argument becomes too much temptation for him. I created The Man with his own tragic flaw—curiosity. This is what keeps him alive and healthy. This insatiable curiosity to learn more than what he should know drives him. It motivates him. It inspires him. It also makes him an addict and vulnerable. Sometimes knowing too much is more dangerous than knowing too little. Sometimes, you aren't meant to know anything at all.

I don't answer him. My wife is indeed receiving the call from her doctor today. And we will find out if she will require surgery, a biopsy, or treatment. I try my best to keep busy in the room, so as to feign anger with The Man. Although he accuses me of being too sensitive with my characters, he too is sensitive to my impression of him.

"If it makes you feel any better, I won't do it again."

Wow, a haphazard apology. My characters must be able to evolve and grow. When I created him, or when he first introduced himself to me as an idea, I never meant to equip him with sensitivity. He was supposed to be the opposite of everything I believed to be good and true. Unlike Kashif, who has more potential to show character from the hole he has dug himself into.

The Man harps upon his sin. The more he talks, the more it sounds like he is confessing to a rape.

"I fell in love with your creation of her. There, I said it. Well, that's not completely true. I fell in lust with your creation of Sabal. I like her sexual aggression and her ability to keep quiet amidst it all. To trust in her ability to show over tell. Very ingenious of you."

Now I sense he is trying to suck up to me. He lays it on.

"I couldn't help myself. I didn't ruin the story, literally. I mean, I made it happen in between the lines, or the way Shakespeare would not stage certain murder scenes, like King Duncan's assassination. It happens off stage. That's it, I made sure to make love to her off stage."

I can see him smirking, or at least craving a manly affirmation of his ability to bed women, albeit fictional in nature. I refuse the spoken word. Like Sabal, I take my vow of silence and rearrange the books on the shelves in order to create a Literacy Section—the new catch word from the Ministry of Education. Improve literacy scores. Standardized testing. No one graduates until they are deemed literate. Educational bureaucrats or Educrats. They don't see how they are destroying the style that must accompany teaching English. It's their subtle attempt to kill it by accident or with the sweep of a broom.

"What? Are you going to hold a grudge because I had sex with one of your characters behind the story's back? Oh, I see. That's it. You're treating her like a daughter of sorts and you wanted me to ask your permission first, didn't you?"

I remain silent. I see why monks resorted to it. It gives me power in this dusty room. It allows me to breathe beyond the block walls.

"She was incredible and I won't apologize for that," he says under his breath.

I pity The Messenger. I shouldn't, I suppose. He doesn't even realize how he got cheated on again. In an attempt to save him the humiliation, I did my best as the author to have Sabal lie to him. The fact these lies make him stronger and allow him the impetus to leave, which I assume, was The Man's first intention before he got his hands on her, is a nice improvisation to move him forward in the story.

"As I said to you before, when you create there is an element of free will to every detail. I acted in free will, that's all. Your God doesn't control you and you certainly don't control me, despite your traditional notions of authorship. Get over it. This is the future. Characters that come alive in between the lines, off the page. Why should that privilege be reserved solely for readers alone and their pathetic interpretations. I bet you don't hold it against them when they interpret your work for another meaning outside of your intent."

He is making much more sense now. I am enjoying the squirming session. It distracts me from thinking about the results of my wife's mammogram, inconclusive as they first were.

I make it look like I am about to tackle another shelf and then I take two quick steps, slap the lights off and close the door behind me. Amidst this most recent enlightenment, The Man deserves some time in the dark.

When I arrive home, my wife is waiting for me in the beautiful scent of tomato sauce percolating on the stove. She is energized and organized preparing dinner with extra special side dishes to compliment the main course, like garlic bread waiting to broil on a baking pan and an antipasto spread already centering the made up table.

"It's only a cyst, formed from a blocked duct and probably caused from Alaia breastfeeding so much."

I run at her and her cheek softens my neck as we embrace.

"I'm going to stick around a little bit more. I hope you don't mind," she whispers in my ear.

I am relieved and there are really no words to express anything original in this moment. I suppose some life experiences, of such importance, require redundant clichés to close them officially. So I use a common one that makes her sigh again in my ear.

"I couldn't do anything without you."

That night we are intimate and excitedly wild after a few glasses of wine. I find myself breathing heavily under a sheath of sweat.

She falls asleep within seconds while I continue to catch my breath. I expect to collapse into a coma, just like her, but the worry hasn't released itself yet.

And it keeps me up half the night, despite the good news.

DAY 18

The Messenger follows the black priest down the hill leading to the hospital from the highway, and up another gravel road. About ten steps behind. To The Messenger it appears as if this priest is not interested in getting to know him. He prefers to walk alone within a certain radius of gravel and bordering cedar forest. The more he walks, the narrower the road gets, the more shaded. It is early in the morning, nearly dawn but it is still night in this valley of historic trees. No signs of life. No stirring. A very tranquil quiet before a rustic stone abode emerges camouflaged just below a rolling hill that flattens at the edge of a cliff.

The possibility of the cliff in his dreams, when he was first assigned his mission, makes his stomach tingle. The Messenger tries hard not to think of Sabal although he wonders about the way she left him. After betraying his trust. In the admission of a lie.

The black priest turns toward the stone shelter. Like Sabal, he leads with his body and not his words. His footsteps are soft, stratospheric, almost above ground. He is not anxious, only patient in his pace. There is no hurry to find warmth or any congenial small talk to make his follower feel at ease. He reaches the wooden door and leaves it open once he enters. Never once glancing back.

In this setting The Messenger is never out of breath. The scent of cedar mixed with a view of the ice caps in the distance, through the trees, on the other side of the cliff, creates a fresh, oxygenated atmosphere. He is invigorated with the air, with the way its sharpness scrapes the edges of his throat. He hesitates before entering not because he is afraid of this strange man, this priest from the hospital. Like the nature surrounding him, he is awakening to the dawn in the most natural way. And his eyes are not strained. They are open and the water within them is loose enough to cry but thin enough to cleanse an infection.

From this valleyed vantage point, the place in the woods resembles the scene he imagined after hearing instructions from The Man in the grotto. It is isolated from the world but close enough to the church in the village, where he was supposed to ask such a priest about Kashif, the person to whom he would deliver his message. Perhaps this is the priest referenced in the initial message, come to lead him to Kashif.

Upon entering, he is surprised to find that the interior of the abode is not as rustic as its exterior. No religious paraphernalia anywhere. Just the black priest sitting in a lazy boy chair by the window overlooking the cliff and its invisible drop. It is a brilliant view of the chasm. There is a white goat outside with his nose in the dirt.

"I assume you have been instructed to find me."

"But *you* found me."

"Yes. I could tell you were looking for me."

"Can you lead me to him?"

He stops. He closes his eyes and his face disappears in the darkened corner.

The living room in which he sits is monastic in presentation. A single chair. No sofa. Nowhere else to sit. No eating table. There is one outside under a fig tree. The white goat poses against this backdrop, looking up every once in a while. The inside area is vacated but for the chair. No television. No portraits or pictures on the walls. The walls themselves are stone, thickened and roughened by mortar. It is cool in this room. The stone hearth is filled with smaller stones as if blockading the chute to prevent the entrance of water.

The priest stands upright. He moves the chair and there is a trap door beneath it.

"Follow me."

The Messenger follows the priest down a ladder which descends loosely in the hollowing depth of an old well. He can hear the echo of water rolling over itself below and like Alice in Wonderland worries of another more colourful world beneath the surface. The priest below him disappears once he reaches the bottom. It is a long descent and surprisingly it is warmer with every step. The inviting scent of something burning climbs up his body as he climbs down the ladder. A web of tangled roots brush up against his face the more he descends and there is no light at his feet. The darkness from below, the sound of water and the rising heat contribute to the disappearance of half of his body. From the waist down he is blind. From the waist up he is disappearing as quickly as the priest.

He trips on the last prong. He sits on clay in the deep hole, in a deeper darkness.

"Stand up and walk."

The instruction echoes.

The Messenger gets up and slams nose first into a clay wall. It is gravelly and dirt enters his mouth. The darkness is suffocating now, as thick as oil.

"Take two steps to the left . . ."

"Ten more steps . . ."

"Five steps to the left again . . ."

"Eight more steps . . ."

"Five more . . ."

"Three more to the left, now five more to the right . . ."

"Take three steps."

Although he has followed every direction, he finds himself in a similar darkened area, more lost in his mind than he was when he first descended the ladder. At least then, there existed the possibility of climbing back up.

"Fall now."

"Fall?"

"Yes, fall."

"How?"

"Fall!"

The Messenger feigns a fall.

"Fall to the ground. No knees."

How does the priest see him in the darkness?

"Get up and fall again."

He does as he is told.

"Place your cheek on the ground."

The Messenger does so.

"Now slide to your left."

The Messenger slides under what appears to be an enormous rock. It is so tight, he begins to hyperventilate. The psychological effect of being buried alive. He breathes in dirt and every time he raises his head it strikes a harder, sharpened surface, until his lips find leather. The foot raises his face from the ground. When he stands, he is nose to nose with the black priest.

And then a door opens. The sound of water echoes loudly as it falls and pools below him somewhere. He follows the footsteps until sensory lights brighten the area slowly, like an artificial sunset.

It is a circular cavern, centered by a pool of water. There is a fishing pole idle by the edge and a stool there.

As the light opens this scene he is focussed on what is before him, the pool of water, how it invigorates his thirst, the sound of it refreshing the air, providing it mist. The priest has disappeared again. The lights soon reveal him in a corner.

"Will you take me to him now?"

The priest walks into a spot lit area. He has a cloth in his hand. He digs his fingernails into his forehead. It is a violent gesture until The Messenger realizes he is removing a wig. When he does so, the shaved scalp is lighter skinned and in contrast to the priest's face. He removes his shirt next to reveal black arms and a black neck but a white chest, completely bare. He becomes naked, two tone in colour, walks over to the inlet of water, dips in the rag and washes himself clean. Before long, he is a naked, hairless man and The Messenger is unsure whether an olive tinge graces the tone of his skin. The priest, or the man no longer purporting the costume of one, walks over to a wall and pushes in a trap door. He returns shortly thereafter in a robe.

"Follow me."

The Messenger ascends the steps to another area, elevated above the water. When he enters the room there are painted portraits on easels, and one with simple, pencil drawings.

On the easels, The Messenger sees depictions of a woman in a full niqab, the blonde-haired man, and the tall brunette from his neighbouring room at the hospital, amongst others. All of them created for the purpose of public disguise. There are new depictions he hasn't seen yet and a rack of costumes. There is also a makeup table with a mirror. A prop area with canes and shoes and accessories. An entire backstage area promoting the assumption of other trap doors and tricks.

"I am the man you are looking for. I am Kashif."

The Messenger is overcome with emotion. His deliverer stands before him and not as a myth or the subject of folklore. He has found the man who will terminate him, the one who will free him from the life that robs him of his dignity. Very naturally, The Messenger approaches him, embraces him, and then kisses him on the cheek once.

"How did you know it was me?" The Messenger asks.

"I have been waiting for this day. I felt you in my dreams. I am sensitive to the silent voices that speak to me. They spoke to me in the hospital."

"But how?"

"How do they speak to me, or how do I hear them?"

"Both."

"They enable me to survive alone. I survive on instinct alone and it has never betrayed me. I don't think. I don't worry. I don't rely on anything but the instincts ingrained in me. I could smell your message. I could sense you were looking for me. I follow my instincts and I never distrust them."

"I almost died before I could tell you."

"But you didn't. This is true. Your survival makes you more invincible."

"Until you kill me yourself."

The Messenger intends this as a hint. Encountering Kashif as a man of pure instinct makes him distrust The Man's promise.

"Follow me."

Kashif walks over to a shelf of books behind the easels. He removes a gun with a silencer. The Messenger's breath accelerates and his nerves adrenalize. He thinks of Sabal. She was his last request, his life's last desire. To experience a connection to the world he had given up on. To enter another human being like a lost soul in search of a temporary temple before ascension.

Kashif dresses in pants, shoes, a loose shirt and jacket. The Messenger follows him outside the backstage area, down the steps, alongside the body of water, across a man-made bridge and to a tiny aperture. When he squeezes through he sees the scene he imagined on the bus in Syria, the one promised to him by The Man in the grotto, his death scene, his last vision—except for the goat. He drops to his knees to revere the fulfilment of this internal apparition. Kashif removes the gun and presses it into the back of his head. The circular point of the gage is infinite, like a moving drill.

"Tell me the message."

"There is a child. He is held captive by a group. He blesses them with health. He cures them of ills, war wounds, even death. He personifies grace and deity, but he cannot walk. This boy needs to be stolen. Only you can breach the walls that imprison him. Only you can find him. By finding him, you will destroy everything you have ever created. By finding him, you will save her. He knows she is your daughter. He has a gun pointed at her neck."

"Who knows my daughter?"

The gun trembles a little and The Messenger doesn't expect this reaction.

"I don't know him. But he knows you. He knows she is your daughter. He seems to know everything. He knows more about me than I know about myself. I don't know him. He wouldn't let me see him. He found me. He asked me to deliver this message. He promised me you would make sure this is my end."

The gun stabilizes again. Finds a flat resting point on the back of his skull.

"Who is this child?"

"A miracle. The next coming."

"Of what?"

"Good?"

"There is no such thing. What if I don't find him?"

"He didn't say."

"Why not?"

"Because he knows you will find him."

"What if I refuse?"

"He didn't say?"

"Why not?"

"He doesn't expect you to refuse."

"What if this boy doesn't exist? This may be a plot to smoke me out of my hole."

"All he said is you would know how to find him."

Kashif loads a single bullet into the gun tunnel. On the ground, The Messenger can feel Kashif stepping back. The balance of the softer ground shifts. The Messenger raises his head like those religious pictures of saints in his grandmother's home. In the midst of angry people setting a young girl on fire, the young girl is looking up to heaven, an aureole of light around her head. The Messenger remembers every one of those pictures of the same theme. The Saint is about to die willingly, just like him, some with smiles or smirks on their faces. Their skin always porcelain, their eyes always blue, their gowns always coloured above the shadowed drabs of their persecutors.

"I'm going to ask you one more time. How does he know my daughter?"

"I don't know. He knows you. He described you perfectly. Your skin. Your face. The way you are going to kill me. The view. He is omniscient."

"Who is?"

"This Man."

Kashif removes the gun from The Messenger's head.

"Get up."

The Messenger turns on his knees and grasps for the gun. He is desperate. He spoke too much, he believes. He distorted the message.

"You need to kill me now. My mission is complete."

"Not to me it isn't."

"You can't do this."

"I do what I want and I need you."

"For what. I am useless to you."

"You will represent me."

"To whom?"

"My captors."

"Your captors?"

"Yes."

"Who are they?"

"We will see soon enough."

"What will we see?"

"Whoever wants me the most? They will have the child."

Day 19

"Have you ever resurrected someone before?"

They return to the area of the cavern that resembles a backstage dressing room. Kashif's question is muffled by the sound of boxes being pushed around in a closeted area. The Messenger waits for him to reappear amongst the circle of easels before he answers.

"What do you mean?"

Kashif is holding a wig in one hand, some crumpled, yellow paper in the other. His face has changed since it first emerged from beneath the made up priest. It transforms in real time. Kashif's face is always transforming in waves of colours, in ripples of skin, every time he moves or says something.

"No one has seen me for fifteen years. They have proclaimed me dead ten times. Every one presumes I am ash. I made myself disappear. I martyred myself, so to speak. We need to make them believe I am who I am."

He raises the wig and is busy arranging other materials. He drags one of the easels from the circle to the center of the room. It is the easel with the pencil drawings. As if in continuous motion, he removes a shard of lead and begins sketching and smudging. The portrait of a man appears like a magic trick performed on the corner of the street in a populated tourist zone. After it is complete, he stretches the other arm out, the one crumpling the yellow papers. The Messenger unravels them to see the replica of the picture aside a news article with the caption "Most Wanted Terrorist Believed Dead."

"This is you?"

"This *was* me."

After he has completed the pencil sketch, he turns it so that it becomes reflected in the mirror by the makeup table.

In a very effeminate manner, Kashif fingers the jars and makeup vials to determine a prescriptive order.

He then takes a seat. Over his left shoulder in the mirror is the drawing. Over his right is an observant messenger.

"Do you know how to take pictures?"

The Messenger nods in a dazed way, as if not hearing the question properly. He watches The Messenger assume a makeup artist posture and it distracts him from words.

"I said do you know how to take pictures?"

"Yes, I do. Why?"

"I need to recreate myself right now. After I do so, with some added years and wrinkles of course, you will take a picture. They will not believe it is me if you show this version. They need to see a version that resembles the pictures in their mosques, those on signs of protest, or others imprinted on candles at cemeteries."

"Where is the camera?"

"In the cove over there, I need to start."

Kashif uncaps the vials and begins painting his face with an assortment of reserved brushes. His touch is delicate, his stroke artistic, and his craft well-learned and articulate in function. Before long, his face is shaded and wrinkled, painted weathered by the hot desert sun. A beard has sprouted thick and grisly on his chin and his eyebrows are thickened and nearly connected at the bridge of the nose. He goes as far as blanching his lips to appear thirsty, or chapped, and even his eyeballs for some reason are yellower.

"Eye drops, that's all." He seems to read The Messenger's confusion.

The final piece is the wild wig with a loose ponytail. When he fastens it securely on his bare scalp it isn't good enough. He disappears behind an easel and behind another cavern wall before reappearing with a spray can. Very expertly he creates layers of grey.

The basics and foundation of his reconstruction resemble the drawing, but the colours and design take into account the lost fifteen years. After he completes the facial, he doesn't ask for an opinion. He doesn't seek any praise for his work either, or criticism.

His creation is as instinctive as his movements, one in the same. He disappears once again behind another easel. They serve so many roles, like doors in front of other doors. Layers of doors.

He returns dressed in dull green military attire with a tattered scarf for his neck. He walks up to The Messenger with a different aura now. And The Messenger is intimidated by the vision, the natural ease of the metamorphosis, the knowledge of what lies beneath the costume, so easily transformative as one in the same. Kashif doesn't say a word because he is biting on his lips to create bruised bubbles beneath the surface, unsmooth landscapes, worn lips. He then drops to his knees as if to kiss The Messenger's feet. The Messenger follows him down with his eyes.

"Kick dirt into my eyes."

"What?"

"I said kick dirt into my eyes."

The Messenger obeys the request. When Kashif rises, his face is dustier than the artificial make up could accomplish. He squints his eyes over and over again to shift the dust around, to make it sting enough. When he opens them, they are blood-shot, embattled.

"Take the camera."

The Messenger removes the lens cap. Even the lens is grainy, as if purposely scratched to create a sepia effect.

Kashif reverses backwards toward the wall. In doing so he finds a place against the cavern not interfered with. A plain back drop for a focused target.

"Hold on. You can't catch me in a pose. It has to appear as if it is a long shot, like someone is spying on me from a distance, unbeknown to me. However, I must appear strong, not like a deer about to be cross-bowed via periscope. No, I want you to start snapping, one after the other. I will change my profile and move my angles, and then we will select the right one not facing the camera, with enough faith in it."

The Messenger takes another step back and aims.

"Start shooting."

The Messenger snaps away. The flash becomes a strobe as he snaps and snaps away with increased speed.

Kashif is not satisfied enough. He changes profiles, he never once looks directly at the camera.

When the camera stalls on its own, he takes it from The Messenger's hands.

Once again, he doesn't ask for an opinion. He wades through the pics with no criticism or appreciation for the photos. He does this for quite some time. Eventually he finds one.

"This one. We will send this one."

"To whom?"

"To the Americans."

"The Americans?"

"Yes. This will cause a holy war here."

The Messenger is confused but after some thought, puts two and two together. A war must start with words before action, internal conflict before external conflict. Insult before injury.

"You want me to send it to a media source."

Kashif freezes his stare. He is not impressed by The Messenger's interpretation of his intentions. Or is he only thinking beyond the step, or listening to his instincts?

"We will send it to a media source, yes, but one here, on the American payroll. An overseas submission will only draw suspicion and disbelief. You will be my agent. You will represent my interests. It must appear like an insult to the American side. My survival will insult them initially, so they will have to take ownership of the story to spin it properly. They will lie, create more story, more fiction, but in doing so, they will accomplish the goal."

"Which is?"

"To make me public to the groups."

"Which groups in particular?"

"The ones funded most by higher economic interests. The most dangerous. One of these interests will reveal which group has the child."

"You are suggesting they come to us."

"Yes. These groups will fight for me. Or over me."

"Why?"

"It will please their employers. It will raise the price of their services."

"Services?"

"Yes. Supply follows demand . . ."

Kashif, or the past version of him, approaches The Messenger on soft footing, as a teacher would a student's desk.

"It is never about religion. It is never about land. It is never about differences. It is never about history. But it is always about eating."

Kashif waves The Messenger on to follow him out of the room.

"Bring the camera with you."

The Messenger does as he is told.

I stop writing because it is late at night and something is happening to me again, or has been happening to me. I don't know what it is. I feel invaded. But it's not The Man this time.

It's hard to describe because I am yet to find the source of it. All I understand is that my body is more difficult to move. My legs are too heavy to run away from my dreams and underneath my skin rows and rows of knives point outward. The overall effect is the sensation of bruising everywhere. Even my face. Underneath my jaw. My entire body, like a sponge, continues to absorb whatever it is without any lightness or release. I've tried to physically exercise it away. I've tried to sleep it away. Perhaps I am tired, or maybe I am burning out trying to balance my four jobs with my four children. But it doesn't feel at all like fatigue, although I lend the condition that excuse.

When my wife found out her lump was benign, a new life entered me, so to speak, to replace the perpetual worrisome one. For a brief moment, I discarded all of my fears of someone closer to me dying the way my cousin died. When he first discovered he had an aggressive form of colon cancer, he didn't tell us, his extended family, that it was deemed terminal. He didn't want to worry his mother, my aunt, or his brothers. For a whole year I held hope he could defeat it. I asked about him often. When I saw him at our annual Christmas party, I assured him we had prayers banked up enough to see him through the ordeal. He and his wife smiled at me. In retrospect, I could tell they knew something more. And that something more was too tragic to reveal at Christmas. And then the truth revealed itself, three months before his death.

He had visited his doctor only to be told never to come back again. The news from the other end of my mother's phone pummelled me. Making matters worse, he didn't want us to see him deteriorate. He wanted to spend his remaining time with his own immediate family. He wanted to spare all of us the horror of his death so we could live on not feeling it for ourselves.

I admired and envied him at the same time. He was a brilliant man with a talent to apply meticulous attention to detail. Someone I aspired myself to be as a writer. He died my age and I felt cheated for never seeing him in this weakened phase of his life. Until the night that he died. We visited my aunt at her home. All of us assembled there to cry and remember him before the official funeral formalities. I remember her house to be so meticulously clean, as if she expected the company at any minute.

It was there that I saw a picture of him, taken recently, before he became bedridden. He appeared so thin, so unrecognizable, so skeletal.

I try to continue the next segment of the story. I am glad I have finally introduced The Messenger to Kashif, although I know The Man will argue I did The Messenger a gross injustice not to kill him off.

I don't understand why I can't think, move, or write without thinking of Tommy. I don't want to mention it to my wife. She will tell me we have everything to be happy about. She will tell me we are lucky and fortunate to have dodged the proverbial cancer bullet. She will question if I love her enough to get past my own, personal issues.

I pour myself a glass of water and it doesn't help. So I sit against the cupboards in a darkened kitchen and shiver.

I have a meeting at work for which The Man counsels me. He considers himself my agent now, I suppose. He must feel really guilty for disrupting the suspension of disbelief in my story. His involvement with one of my minor characters, Sabal, is a direct violation of our trust and it further harms the traditional order of being between creator and the created.

"Don't worry about the meeting. It isn't something to fret over. You can quit this job and make a living from your writing, you know."

This shot of tequila confidence in me burns my throat as I drive in to school again. I have the radio on and the sky is too white this morning to hold anything colourful within it. The Man tries to speak louder than the music. It is a Sinead O'Connor song that I secretly like and never admit to anyone else. The one Prince wrote, "Nothing Compares 2 U." I don't know why I continue to like this song about a broken relationship, since mine is stronger than ever after hearing the news of my wife's benign cyst. The song speaks to me in subtle ways and I appreciate the simplicity of the images. The sadness lies in this confessional simplicity.

The Man doesn't understand that his overstated attempt to gain my better side again is interfering with my connection to the song. I'm not in the mood to argue with him. He can talk, and although I try not to listen, I do.

"So your principal has called a meeting with your union leader to discuss a coffee run on your lunch break?"

I don't say anything. I know what The Man is implying. I don't want to engage, even though he is volunteering to be my friend in this professional matter. He doesn't understand I would prefer to be just that, professional, through and through in my career. And he isn't a part of this career path, although he has interfered mightily in the other. My day job is separate from him, as it is separate from the friends I grew up with, or my extended family. It's another world they don't belong in, another one The Man doesn't belong in, although he wishes to stake claim in it.

"So you're going to use the professional card? Professionalism is a good looking wall to hide behind, so stop making excuses for what you are dying to say."

I ignore him, although I wish his support could make me feel better. The Man isn't as selfish as I thought. Why invest this energy in my real career conflicts? Maybe he is sincerely concerned. Or, he has discovered another agenda to launch his character back into the story. Perhaps he feels threatened himself after I kept The Messenger alive. That pushes him to a third bidding automatically. The Man keeps sliding down the bench in the story and I know he values his character above everyone else's, even Kashif's, my protagonist.

It is work to hide these thoughts from him now. I have taught myself to think about two things at once to disguise them. As I drive into school and wait in the traffic line again, I think about the Facebook messages my deceased cousin's wife posts on occasion. She really misses him. She suffers thinking about him. I know he wouldn't want her to, but she does so anyway. She laments about friends trying to comfort her from the comfort of their own tragic free lives. No one could possibly understand what she is going through and words are never good enough to change a person's tragic state of mind. I've learned that on my own. And despite what I want to hear as I attend this meeting intended to reprimand me, that the accusation of fetching a coffee on my lunch break is ridiculous, it will do very little to free me from my self-imposed pressure. I am heavy again. Weighted in my shoes. Sore in my arms. Every once in a while, I feel random pains in my neck and shoulders. And I don't feel like teaching anymore.

I feared this day would come when I first started out. I expend so much energy in each class. I often transform into a cartoon for my lower level readers so they can stay attentive. I

become a stand-up comedian in other classes to entertain them
into learning or grasping otherwise boring curriculum demands.
All the while, I worried that the energy would run out one day.
How could I have guessed, I would learn to hate the sound of
my own voice.

"You are a great teacher. Your students admire you. Your
colleagues emulate you. Without conflict, air doesn't clear. Good
things come from these types of tests."

The Man's voice is self-help now. He must recognize me
drowning before I realize I am in deeper waters than I thought.

"Like you?" I tease.

"Please give me better credit than that. You created me for
God's sake."

I pull into the parking lot and I find it difficult to pull my
bags out of the truck. Even such a menial chore in its daily rep-
etition feels like work to my body. I spite the routine of every
day, although it will find disruption with my meeting during last
period.

By the time I reach my classroom, I have avoided all social
contact. I pride myself on not bringing baggage into my classroom. I advise my students to do the same. I treat it as hallowed
ground. They still don't see it, but humour me nonetheless. And
yet here I am, lugging a truckload full of it today. My students
smell hypocrisy like blood hounds so I try my best to escape this
source-less depression.

As if timed to lend me extra-terrestrial help from the uni-
verse, a coincidental email comes my way. The timing is too
uncanny. It is too intended, almost overly contrived.

I read this random email from the Loran Scholarship
Foundation. Our first Loran Scholar graduate from our school
nominated me for a teaching award and the email outlines that
my principal has been advised of the future presentation. It makes
me laugh. It is all too obvious.

I search for The Man in the room. This has his fingerprints
carbonized all over it. He is nowhere to be found, which makes
him the prime suspect. My students are filing in.

"What is it, sir?" Nico asks me.

"Nothing, why?"

"Your tie doesn't match your shirt. Did you change in the dark again?"

"You got it, Nico."

I walk out into the hallway, not caring if the vice principal is lurking in the stairwell corridor expecting to arrest me for not being in my classroom before the anthem and prayer announcement. The Man is nowhere to be found.

I return to my desk and re-read the email. It is a national award and I am honoured by the quote taken from Aaron's nomination essay. I want to cry, but not because I am honoured. I feel so undeserving, so tricked.

The Man sits in the desk next to Emily, my human grey hair detector.

"I have nothing to do with it. It's not just a coincidence. And I didn't know about it either. I meant everything I said and the email is proof for my words."

I continue to ignore him to imagine the principal's reaction.

I have three good classes in a row after receiving my award email. I find myself laughing again amongst my students and it doesn't feel forced or unnatural. I deliver my lessons very smoothly with comedic grace and focus. By the time my preparatory period arrives, the Union leader is waiting for me outside the main office door.

"Are you ready?"

"Yes."

"Is there something else I should know before we go in? Does she have something more than you grabbing a coffee?"

"Not that I know of," I smile.

"I hear you are the recipient of a national teaching award, congratulations." He offers me his thick hand and I shake it. His smile is fatherly. He is a retired teacher himself with white hair but much thicker bodied than The Man I imagined for my story. His blue eyes crease like they are pitying me at the same time.

"Okay, let's go in then."

I follow Terry in through the office and the secretaries who often tease and flirt with me whenever I am waiting for a fax or to see an administrator, are quiet in their concern. When we arrive to the office, the principal, Mrs. Smith, and Mr. Lye, are waiting. Absent is the vice principal with whom I get along.

Mrs. Smith shakes hands with Terry. Mr. Lye is seated at the round table with a notebook already scribbled upon.

"Hi, Dean. Just received the email from the Loran Foundation. Congrats on the award. I hear that maybe the Governor General will present it."

"Thank you," I say.

Terry is surprised by my principal's open recognition of me. He has ferreted every foul intention from this principal and is temporarily stunned to find her the bigger person from the start.

We take a seat and the vice principal has his head down. He is writing. I look in his direction as if to wait for him to stop.

The principal raises her glasses to the perch of her nose before handing me a printed paper under the school's letterhead. Terry quickly asks for a copy and is provided one as well.

"I am filing this letter with Human Resources. It details how you went for a coffee on your preparatory period. It also points to how you said to Mr. Lye, "you handle things your way."

The Man is sitting at the principal's desk, in her leatherback lounge chair. He snuck himself in somehow, without my detection.

"Call her on it," he advises me.

"Hold on," I say. "I said no such thing and it has been taken entirely out of context. I was asked by Mr. Lye how I handle late assignments. I explained to him that my way is to follow the Growing Success document and to allow opportunities to submit to a certain point in time, whereby I determine if the assignment is deserving of a no mark, or a zero. I did not say it that way."

The vice principal does not answer or raise his head. He is writing everything down.

"Good for you," The Man says. His voice is condescending from the principal's chair. I don't appreciate being in an inferior position with one of my created characters. Ironically, I don't feel this way before my principal and vice principal, or my union leader. I feel justified by my innocence.

"Hold on," Terry settles me down with a hand.

"You are writing him up because he went to get a coffee on his break, down the street, on a Friday afternoon. May I ask who saw him getting the coffee?"

"I did," my principal answers. She removes her glasses and assumes a more erect sitting posture. The spaces in between her fingers are red, her ring on the marriage finger unpolished gold with a sharp rocky summit.

"What were you doing in the Starbucks, if I may ask?"

"Getting coffees for the office."

"So you are writing him up and filing this in Human Resources?"

"He is not supposed to leave the school on his prep period."

"Do other teachers go down the street to grab a coffee on their prep period?"

"Yes, I'm sure they do," my principal answers.

"Then why are they not in this room with us today."

"Because he was caught."

Terry chuckles a little to himself. The Man sitting in the principal's seat is not laughing.

"This is your day job?" The Man asks me. His sarcasm is annoying.

Mr. Lye, the vice principal, continues to write, as if inspired.

"Isn't that a double standard?"

"No it isn't. He knows the rules."

"But you just said other teachers do it."

"That's not the issue here."

I listen to the tennis exchange in this conversation and I zone out. I think about The Messenger and Kashif, stranded in the last chapter of my story. They wait for me patiently, as if preferring to exist in the fictional world I have created for them. Despite its violence, its heartbreaking juxtapositions, and the steep challenges presented before them, the world I have created is ironically far more real and far less absurd than the one I currently exist in. How would you justify a scene like illegally retrieving a coffee on a break, in a novel, I ask myself. I'm not sure it would sustain any suspension of disbelief. A principal arguing with a

teacher's union leader about a teacher who went out on his
break, like so many others in the course of a week of work do,
to grab a coffee? And the best part about it is I went with someone else, who is not being written up. Better yet, I'm not a coffee
addict like this friend of mine from Special Ed. I was driving to
London later in that day to pick up my son and I usually have a
coffee to keep me awake on the three-hour drive, which is the
only reason I agreed to go.

"Fiction is far more real than reality," The Man follows my
train of thought. "With fiction, you crave making sense of a situation. In reality, no situation makes sense enough to crave."

"I think you are enjoying this moment too much," I finally
speak directly to him with my mind's voice.

"Of course I am. You shouldn't be here. Yes, you are a good
teacher and your students adore you. You found your calling.
You found your means by which you give back to your commu-
nity. If they gave out medals for such service, you would be
highly decorated. But this routine is killing you. Can't you see
that? You work harder every year and you don't get a raise.
You've topped off on the pay grid. The guy who teaches next to
you, strike that, the guy who never teaches in the room next to
you, makes the same and he isn't in this office wasting his time.
He flies under the radar. Hell, he even gets to have coffee or
breakfast on his prep period, like everyone else. It may be time
for you to think about your life. You are having a mid-career cri-
sis, and we need you more."

I never thought of my characters as needing me as much as
my students do on a daily basis. It isn't too farfetched, is it? My
characters are as broken as many of my students. They need their
creator to animate them in the same way I animate Shakespeare
for a student who will never appreciate it enough to see it performed live with a future love interest. Yes, it is nice to receive
cards that note how I inspired this student, or opened new doors
of understanding for another. But don't my characters need to be
inspired as well? Or do they only get leftover inspiration energy
at the end of a day, or in the eye-crusted hours of the early, darkened morning?

The argument has provoked raised voices.

Terry finally stops it before it twists out of control.

"All of Dean's evaluations are sparkling and just today he was informed he will receive a national teaching award. We will take this letter with us."

Terry rises from his seat and pulls me by the arm to do the same. We are not very synchronized in making body language statements.

"Good day."

He lets me walk out of the office first and we reconvene in the foyer before the main entrance to the school.

"We will file this with our previous paperwork as an attempt at a retaliation for your first grievance and present it before the trustees."

I'm not really listening to him. Instead, I wonder if The Man remained in the office to listen in on the principal's private, aftermath meeting with the vice principal.

"Dean, is everything all right?"

"Yes, sorry Terry. Thanks for everything."

"I think you are the first one in history to be written up for getting a coffee on his break. Congratulations."

I smile.

"I'll get back to you soon. Keep your head up, kid. That's a nice award."

I watch him leave the school and consider quitting my job for the first time.

"Okay, we need a believable story for the past fifteen years."

Kashif has led The Messenger out onto the cliff again. The sun has brightened the sky. Kashif is picking vegetables from his garden as he thinks aloud. As he uproots them, they dangle colourful in his grasp.

"How about we begin with the real one," The Messenger interrupts, drawing an ireful look from Kashif.

"I mean. Knowing the true story will allow us to create a fictional one, no?"

"I knew it was wrong to kill you. Okay, let us eat first."

Kashif takes the vegetables to a well, disguised by an area in the bush on a cliff. He ropes up a basin and cleanses them thoroughly. He then delivers them to the picnic table.

"I haven't eaten meat since I found her," he begins.

He pushes a pink beet in The Messenger's direction. It is sour but his hungry mouth adapts to its freshness.

"I created terror, if you need to know. I mean, terror has always existed. Fear has always existed, and leaders have always exploited it to govern and rule. But I organized terror. I made it a commodity and this commodity made many a man rich. I found ways to sell it to the highest bidder, and in doing so, I owned a share in it. Terror is a product now."

Kashif bites on a narrow carrot. Without swallowing it, he bites on a celery stalk and a deep green herb.

"The secret," he says, "is to mix the raw vegetables in your mouth. The unison improves the palate and vitaminizes your blood."

He takes a flask from a pocket.

"Here, have some."

The Messenger drinks, all the while thinking it is poison until he remembers how cursed he is to live forever with a sarcastic desire to die.

He nearly chokes. It is thick oil.

"It's a mixture of fresh pressed olive oil and seed oil. It needs to be cold crushed for the right fats to escape."

The Messenger quickly pulls another leafy stem his way to eliminate the sticky taste in his mouth.

"When I was a young boy, I lived a death wish like you. My father died as a soldier fighting for the wrong cause. For justice, he always told my mother. For our people, he always told me. I saw him as a hero until he died. And then, I kept forgetting him. Over and over again, I tried hard to remember him. I kept his sepia picture by my bedside. But time made him disappear for me. Because he died, my mother starved to death to keep me and my brother alive. Right here, in Lebanon. She picked olives for me. She stole figs. She sold herself for anything she could put in my mouth. And I fed from her, selfishly. My brother and I, both. He was younger than me but I couldn't help myself some days. I often thought I could eat him if things got worse. It was then, we were stolen away."

"You were kidnapped?"

"Yes, but my mother knew. She didn't object. She accepted we might eat some more from another hand. We left her sick and dying on her own. At the very least, we could climb trees for her. Hunt little animals. Build a fire. But this man in a uniform took us away. She didn't resist him. She waved and that was the last I saw of her.

"The military man in green took us to a camp with other boys. There, he fed us beyond our imagination. Everything from figs to meat to cedar berries. Even imported delicacies, like Baklava. We grew fat stomachs, my brother and I, at this camp, and we had fun learning how to shoot a gun and a bow and arrow. I never once thought about my mother. Or my father. The Military Man was our hero, our father and our mother. We waited to see him every day. He held candies in his pockets for us. We were not even seven years old yet. He liked us above all of the others, we believed. He pretended to hold special treats for us that he didn't give to the others. And then he disappeared. I mean, the body remained, but that generous man disappeared. Overnight."

"Overnight?"

"Yes. He came to us the next day. When we put out our hands he burned them with his cigarette. When we moved to embrace him with a grateful gesture, he kicked us in the face. My brother lost teeth. I broke my nose. He spat on us. He peed on us. He shit on us one day while others held our faces down in the bedrock.

"And then he reappeared like a magic trick. The same man. The same body, but a different face, a different personality, a different character, a different voice. I didn't know how to see him without fearing the bad version would return. I never trusted him again. I couldn't. He had burned me. He had raped me. He had hurt my brother and I and now he was helping us again, feeding us again, kissing us again. It was Jekyll and Hyde but in the same place and in the same clothes. We feared which man would approach us the next morning.

"After he had fattened us up again, he began speaking to us alone. My brother was younger and he followed me everywhere until this Military Man divided us. My brother cried. He was hardened by our lives but still sensitive to pain. For some unknown reason, I taught myself how to freeze over, how to become numb to it all. This Military Man spoke to us in a dark room with no light. I could only hear his voice in the darkness. I couldn't tell if it was Jekyll or Hyde, but every time, he pushed me to be honest with him.

'Do you miss your mother?'

'No.'

'Do you miss your father?'

'No.'

'Do you hate your mother?'

'Yes.'

'Why?'

'Because she couldn't take care of me.'

'Do you love your brother?'

'Yes.'

'Do you want to take care of him?'

'Yes.'

'Even if he eats more and you eat nothing.'

'No.'

'Who do you think I am?'

'The Devil?'

'Is the devil as generous?'

'Yes.'

'Do you like pain?'

'How do you know?'

'You smile when I hurt you.'

'It feeds my stomach. I am not hungry afterwards.'

'You will change the world.'

No answer.

'You will change the world.'

"I didn't know what that meant, what he meant. I assumed he asked the others the same questions, but now I don't believe so. I think he asked us different questions. I think he was not human. He was a man all right, but one I couldn't see in the ease in which he killed compassion. He seemed created from a story, from a fable. His face changed every day. It was never the same face."

The Messenger considers the irony in this statement because Kashif doesn't seem aware he appears the same way to him. The more Kashif explains or relates his story, the more it sounds like an apprenticeship. The sky is cerulean blue again and the peaks on the mountains are artificial white, newly painted and outlined against their backdrop. Kashif doesn't speak directly to him. He speaks to the sky, as if connecting it to a floating audience or one elevated in a theatre.

"The other boys didn't talk. I wondered why. They kept their mouths closed. They never conversed with one another, or with my brother and me. It was strange to me, to see boys, around fifty of us, not conversing. I assumed they were told not to speak, or they were afraid to be punished for it. One day, a boy attacked us in the wood shed that we slept in. All of us slept separately, in tiny, wood sheds. He jumped on my brother and I strangled him until he couldn't breathe. When his life expired, his mouth gaped open and I realized he didn't possess a tongue. It had been carved out, expertly.

"I didn't let my brother see. If he saw, the very sight of this boy's blackened mouth would horrify him. Instead, I dragged the body out but I didn't want to hide it. I wanted to show it off to the Military Man. So I left him in the middle of the camp. Although I couldn't see him anywhere, I knew the Military Man would approve.

"Days and months passed and the numbers dwindled in the camp. More and more boys disappeared. We exercised. The Military Man fed us well. He allowed only my brother and I to stay in the wooden shed together. No other boys were allowed to bunk. I assumed we were the only blood brothers.

"One day, everyone disappeared entirely. No boys, no Military Man. Just my brother and I abandoned in the camp. We didn't know what to do. We didn't know where to go. So we stayed and waited. We waited to be told what to do. No one came for three days. We didn't eat. We didn't enter the compound of the camp. We were too wary of it being a trick. We craved food and for the first time, I thought about eating my own brother. The thought crossed my mind and I fought it over and over again. After the third night, everyone reappeared again. The remaining tongue-less boys and the Military Man. He was quiet to us for an entire week. He didn't say a word and I wondered if he had lost his tongue as well. I wondered if we would be next in this army of tongueless soldiers.

"We continued to train our bodies physically, but not military training. It resembled the exercises animals performed to keep their instincts sharp. We climbed trees, practiced balance on branches, fell from those branches in an attempt to land softly, like a cat. When The Military Man resumed his instruction to the camp, he taught us how to use our teeth. He said our teeth were strong in their roots. That they could bite through anything, even the bark of a cedar. So we broke bark with our teeth. We hunted with our teeth.

"The Military Man released a possum in the camp area and we had to hunt it down with our teeth, kill it with our teeth, and then deliver it to him with our teeth. I won every battle. My brother didn't even try. Others tried to bite me while I hunted but I withstood them every time. And the Military Man appreciated my victories. He could see how I outsmarted the others. How I lured my prey expertly, waiting for the others to draw him in my direction, until I pounced on it myself.

"The others soon relented to my dominance over them. They kept disappearing, one by one, as if shipped off to other parts of the world in a package. I never asked about them. I knew questions would bother the Military Man. I knew they would make him go away. After a while, I waited for him like a boy expects his father coming home from work in the evening.

"Before long, it was only my brother and I left in the camp. He had also strengthened. He didn't cry anymore at night. His nightmares subsided. The look in his eye was cold and icy and no longer soft and childlike. I would catch him staring at me now like he didn't recognize me anymore. I couldn't see myself but I assumed I had changed to him as well. I had become someone different, like the Military Man, except I hadn't learned how to control it yet like him.

"We ate and became strong, but we spoke less and in whispers. Our actions spoke for us. The Military Man didn't test us against each other, for obviously, I would win, although he did train us both. We hunted birds in the trees like cats. For weeks we practiced this impossible exercise. At the beginning, I was never close, but each day, I came closer and closer to entrapping one. My brother never progressed in this exercise. He was always too slow, or ever too obvious. Or maybe he never believed he could do it. But I did. I knew I could accomplish this impossible challenge. It would make me undisputed, even to the Military Man.

"When I accomplished the feat finally, I had never felt so surreal to myself. I crept up on a bird sitting on a branch. Without thinking, my instincts calculated the rush of my attack on a narrow branch, knowing full well, I would risk falling in this attempt. That was it. I was never prepared to fall for the attack.

Mind you, the both of us did when we tried. But before trying, I had never accepted the fall as being part of the attack. So on this early morning, while the bird fluttered its wings on the branch, I moved stealth-like on all fours until I smacked it with my hand. In the process, I fell from the high branch but not without grabbing the stunned bird in my hand first. I adjusted my body during the fall and rolled over onto my side with the balance of a cat, the bird in my hand, whose spasms attempted to escape the violent grip of my squeezing grasp. The Military Man saw the bird squirming there, losing strength. He didn't have to tell me what to do. My brother seemed to know what I was about to do, so I crushed it some more before I placed it entirely in my mouth."

The Messenger believes himself to be the little brother in this scene, for some reason. He sees himself in that character's role, watching his brother become a virtual animal before him, and then hunting down an innocent bird, before eating it in a more violent conclusion. As Kashif is lost in the story, The Messenger is captivated by his face. In waves, like a body of water conducted by weather systems, it flattens out peacefully at times, before it ripples with a jolt of wind. Kashif doesn't see himself now, in the same way he didn't see himself then. It is all about the change, The Messenger thinks, and Kashif is once again transforming into his former self, the one hidden by all of his disguises, the version he never wanted his daughter to see. Or so The Messenger assumes.

"Did you kill him?" The Messenger asks.

"Who?"

The question stuns Kashif out of his trance.

"Your brother? He must have been the last test, the one that completes the metamorphosis."

"Yes. After I became a predator, the Military Man didn't even have to ask me to. I strangled him in his sleep, while he slept. He didn't wake. Maybe in his dreams he expected me to kill him in this peace. I knew it was coming. My instincts informed me I would find the Military Man outside our wood shed the next morning, holding a rifle with one bullet lodged in the canister. I understood he would hand me the gun, so my

instincts beat him to the punch. But there was still one more lesson to learn."

Kashif turns from The Messenger and away from the mountains, as if to look around the corner of his man-made garden.
The white goat has sauntered away, as if afraid of this plot point
in the story.

"A predator doesn't kill for sport. A predator kills to eat,"
The Messenger translates Kashif's look.

"I haven't seen the Military Man since. He disappeared for
good after having trained me."

"What did you do then?"

"I lived a life of instinct, that's what I did."

The Messenger is surprised to find he is no longer hungry for
meat. He understands now why he will never crave it again.

Day 22

The Messenger finds himself in the cavern again. This time, he is fishing alongside Kashif.

"Now that I know the true story, we must make up a fictional one that is believable in its narrative perspective," suggests The Messenger.

Kashif nods. He doesn't eat the fish that hook on his line. And there are many that do. He unhooks them and places them gently in the water. The Messenger finds it difficult to catch one. Kashif never offers him one to eat.

"The stories must co-relate. You were trained to live a life of instinct. You created groups that sold terror. And then you disappeared after finding your daughter. How did you find her?"

"Her mother."

Kashif treats the fishing exercise like a yoga ritual. It is fluid and he breathes out loud with every cast. After a while, he stands up, places the rod next to the stool and walks in the direction of the backstage area at the top of the stone stairs.

"We have to make costumes now."

The Messenger follows him up the stairs. Behind another easel, Kashif rolls out a sewing machine.

"Help me with the fabric."

The Messenger is led to another area with stacked rolls of fabric sparkling with embedded metallic accents. He walks over to one and feels its clean smoothness.

"Silk. The finest," Kashif explains. "I think we should wear dark blue."

"Dark blue?"

"Yes. For our meeting."

"With whom?"

"You will see. Help me with the roll."

The Messenger grabs one end and Kashif lifts the other. Kashif then transforms into a tailor. He removes a measuring tape from his pocket.

"Stand with your legs apart."

After taking his measurements without writing anything down, Kashif goes to work with scissors. He doesn't ask for help. He is busy and he doesn't want to be disturbed.

"Do you need any help?"

"With what?"

"With what you are doing?"

"No, it will not take me long. And then we will hike up the mountain."

"Hike?"

"Yes. You can prepare your statement to the network there, the one where you will reveal me."

"We don't have the story yet. Where you have been for the past fifteen years."

"We will discuss it on the hike."

"What are you making?"

"A suit. It will fit you like another layer of skin."

Kashif buries his head as close as he can get his eye to the pumping needle, which is manually controlled by his foot. He tests its ability to puncture. The Messenger walks away to observe the easels in more detail. They depict caricatures in costume. Kashif is an artist, a fashion sketch artist emerging from his own designs. The attention to detail is both imaginative and precise. On another wall are landscapes and scenes. Memories. Some of them are violent. Others are long perspectives on wars.

"I paint my memories," Kashif speaks without breaking his concentration.

"They reconcile my sins."

Exhausted by the stress of the day, The Messenger manages to sit down against the cavern wall. He falls asleep and is woken by the smell of new fabric run through the marriage of thread and electricity.

Kashif is now dressed in a new power suit, a bone white shirt and a golden tie. He is preparing his tie as if for an interview.

"Try yours on."

The Messenger sees his suit on another stool with a freshly pressed shirt on top and a silver tie.

"I don't have time to stitch buttons, so you will have to use those."

A handful of pearls rest in a pile on top of the shirt. They look like teeth, or ivory pieces, bone chunks, but they are perfect spheres.

"I had some left over from another costume."

The Messenger dresses in his suit and finds a place next to Kashif in the mirror. They are of similar height. The Messenger's hair has grown longer and lighter on this journey, while Kashif is completely bald with no traces of stubble or a former hairline.

"What about shoes?"

"I have some."

"You made the shoes too?"

"No, I have saved many gifts."

Kashif leaves the mirror and The Messenger is surprised to find how well the suit becomes him. He can't remember the last time he wore a suit to look this formal. Perhaps his wedding. Or his son's baptism.

"You are size ten, no?"

Kashif places brand new shoes from the box in front of The Messenger's feet.

"I have many more if you don't prefer these."

The Messenger nods to assure Kashif they are fine.

Kashif is satisfied enough to return the sewing machine to its storage place. The fabric roll is cleanly tied together and ready to be stored as well.

There is a sketch drawing on one of the easels. It depicts Kashif and The Messenger standing in front of a mirror with their suits. The Messenger is amazed by how Kashif makes his visions come to life so easily, so quickly.

"We will hike in these suits?"

"No. I have suit bags for them. We will hike in the proper attire. We will use the suits once we are brought before the council."

"The council?"

"Yes."

"I will not ask."

The Messenger realizes he doesn't need to know everything before he does it with Kashif. Kashif's instincts are trustworthy to The Messenger. He believes in them. He is able to live within their protection, as long as he doesn't cross the line to become an enemy of them.

Kashif waves The Messenger into an elongated change room, which resembles a perfectly carved box from stone. He removes hiking boots and other costumes. Kashif decides to wear a cloak and turban. He offers The Messenger neutral, camouflage attire, as one would find on a reporter freelancing in dangerous war zones.

"You will interview me once we arrive at the mountain, away from here. I do not want to endanger the people of this village or risk exposing the hospital. They will expect me to have hid like a prophet in a cave, on the mountain. You will be my agent. You will represent me to the network. I will not speak to anyone directly, except through you. This will keep you safe from harm. We will discuss my story further when we reach the mountain."

Kashif prepares some more provisions, some warmer clothes, makeup vials, instruments to apply them expertly, and he finds the oldest bag in the closet to stuff them into. He pulls out a lead box from which he removes a tiny, lock and key box. There are needles and narrow flasks inside. He closes it shut and stuffs it into the bag, as well as a phone.

"We must take Gibran with us."

"The goat?"

"Yes. Who will feed him?"

When they reach the surface again, Kashif cuts the goat loose and it follows him like a dog without distraction or the dependence on a leash. The Messenger once again is amazed by the goat's obedience.

Kashif places the bag on the goat's back and ties it securely around its belly. The goat waits like a donkey and looks Kashif in the eye until he is finished, as if trying to please him. Without saying a word, Kashif walks away from the stone abode and the goat tiptoes in his master's footsteps.

The Messenger follows from a distance knowing it isn't time yet to learn more.

DAY 23

"This Kashif is quite the character, if I do say so myself," The Man gloats as if assuming responsibility for Kashif's evolving creation. I am eating lunch alone at school. My lunch period extends into my prep period and I wait until the first lunch period is over to gain this quiet time to think to myself.

"He is the story now," I say. I lose interest in my lunch now that I know The Man is in the room expecting my attention. I worry sometimes that I am speaking aloud to him. I wouldn't want anyone to enter the staff room and overhear a conversation I am having with myself. It is only now that I consider the fact I may be having a nervous breakdown. All of the symptoms are there. I crave sleep more than I ever have in my life, and yet when it is time to sleep, I can't. When I do eventually fall asleep, I wake up at the same times every morning, 2:11AM and 4:17AM. It makes me feel like my body is controlling my mind, or my ability to control it.

I am only free when I am teaching or writing. I suppose these distractions afford me an escape from over-thinking about previous conversations. Perhaps they tame my fruitless searches for higher meaning, which only seem to bury me deeper into myself.

I look for places to be alone but I fear being absolutely alone, physically and mentally, for various reasons. My panic attacks, the ones that haunted me as a child and teenager, have returned with greater intensity. Every time I wake in the night I am out of breath. I can't stop thinking of losing everything, of another tragic event happening to me, how I am inviting such an event by over-thinking it—how I may deserve it in the end.

And now I am sick enough in my stomach to have bouts of vomiting and diarrhea, strained vision, sore ankles and muscles and dry lips.

I punch these symptoms into the internet at an obsessive rate. They are linked to so many terminal endings, but also to many menial, seasonal cold and flu ailments.

"If writing cures you of these ills, quit your job and do what you want to do. It's not that hard. Let those babies starve a little. Your kids are too spoiled anyway."

The Man is alluding to my two sons. The one who lives apart from me and my six-year-old. Both of them are under-achieving in school. Both of them seem to have attitude issues or inabilities to focus and apply themselves.

I nearly struck my six-year-old the other day. My wife signed him up for an indoor soccer camp on Sundays. With other kids his age and younger, they run through drills and fitness games. He has fun in the drills and he is happy and playful. But when the scrimmage starts he is screwing around with a few of his friends. He is trying to entertain them with "poop" jokes and "fart" sounds. He does this often with our son Tobias during bath time. Although Tobias is nearly five, his mind is equitable to a two-year-old's, so he laughs hysterically. But no one is laughing on the soccer pitch. The coach is upset. He is constantly remind-ing Oscar to seek out the ball. He doesn't move in any predes-tined direction. Younger kids run right by him with the ball without his acknowledgment of their existence. And then he cheers when the other team scores on his net.

I understood this behaviour when he was four, and tolerated it when he was five, but now that he is six, it raises heartburn in me. Sitting uncomfortably on this smelly, turf field, and watching other kids run by my son who is showing no interest or focus again disturbs me beyond the limits of my own temper. I ignore everything my wife is saying to me.

"Can you be more social with the parents? You look miser-able," she whispers.

She is right. I am miserable. I have never been one to project my own aspirations onto my son, but he isn't even trying. I am watching him in a wide open view misbehave, goof off, and not even break a sweat. So I snap at my wife.

"He is too spoiled," I growl under my breath.

"We don't buy him anything."

"Everyone else does. But that's not what I mean. He is spoiled with attention. And when he doesn't get it in spades, he starts searching for it, and it only."

"He's just a kid," my wife reasons. I can tell she is fearing my words.

"Then why is he the only one not going after the ball. He is playing soccer today, not entertaining kids on recess. He has no focus."

"I knew you shouldn't have come. Don't talk to me."

She says this with a strained, disguising smile for the other parents. They aren't even listening to our conversation. If they were, they would think I was one of those fathers who thinks his son will play professional sports one day. I'm not. I don't care about sports and I never aspired to those lofty goals. And God knows, I am not one to live vicariously through another, unless it is one of the characters I create in a story. But I do want my kids to try. I want them to work hard at everything they do. I don't want them to act entitled. And I don't want them to be spoiled. I want them to transcend and be original unto themselves, which is why my wife is angry with me. We had an argument the week before about my son attending too many birthday parties. According to my wife, if you invite a friend from his class, you have to invite everyone not to leave anyone out, or ostracize. So my son will attend twenty-two parties this year! I thought the idea was ludicrous since some of these parties happen on the same day.

"Don't you dare say you didn't grow up this way again!" was how the argument ended on her note of disgust. But I couldn't disagree with her more. I don't want my kids following the flow of this insanity. If a kid in his class doesn't want to invite him to a party, he shouldn't go—period.

So I take it out on my six-year-old son on the way home. My tone of voice scares my wife and I know, while I am lecturing him, that the boomerang effect will return to strike me in the back of the head with less sleep and more guilt.

"You don't want to play, then you're not playing anything anymore!" I scream from the front seat. In the rearview mirror, he is frozen in his booster seat. He has to wear glasses now, since one of his eyes is weaker than the other, which makes me feel a whole lot guiltier for some reason. But he isn't blind, and I'm not finished.

"You are nothing but a goof! That's all. You goof off and no one is laughing! Can't you see that! They were playing soccer and you were goofing off all by yourself. Because that's all you are, a goof! My son is a goof!"

He isn't crying. He isn't moving. He doesn't like this tone of voice.

"No more stories before bed. If you want a story, you are going to read it yourself. You are six years old and you don't read on your own yet! No more cuddles, and so help me God if you cry for one more stupid reason, I will give you more to cry about."

My wife is shocked by my tone of voice and the sharp edge to my words. She knows not to interrupt me or maybe I have frightened her as well.

"And no more treats for nothing!"

These are my last words. Even the radio volume has lowered due to my voice. During the remainder of the ride, I think how ridiculous I sounded. No treats? Really? This is how I father? My wife doesn't say anything and when we finally park in the drive-way, I have more to say.

"You are going to hang up your coat! You are going to work every day now if you can't play right. You will clean dish-es, you will scrub floors, you will clean up your brother's mess, you will do everything you never want to do!"

My son leaves the car sullen. When he enters the house he nearly skips with speed to hang up his coat. He can't even reach the pole to hang his jacket but he rushes to the bathroom to get the toilet stool. He then rushes downstairs to the toy room to clean up the mess.

My wife is about to defend him but I put my hand up.

She is more shocked to see this method of Gestapo control.

I whisper, "He is soft and he acts like a little baby. He tattle-tales, he sucks out, and he doesn't listen. It's my turn to fix him."

"Fix him?"

"Let me be his father," I say, as if to blame her for something otherwise.

She walks away.

That night, when he goes to bed, I stand at the doorway making sure she doesn't take his side. I know she agrees with the need to change his behaviour, but she completely abhors the manner in which it was introduced.

I can hear him whisper to her, "I'll try harder to be good, Mommy."

It breaks my heart instantly, and now my heart seems to break over and over again as if by default. Every time I think of my deceased cousin. Every time I consider how ungrateful I am for not appreciating my wife's good health news. Every time I teach my lower level readers and hear their broken family stories. Every time I see Tobias struggling to walk in his cast ankle shoes. Every time I see him eating baby food from a pouch. Every time I think about what my estranged son is doing. His misbehaviours. My inability to help him from a distance.

"I told you feeling sorry for yourself would only lead to your ruin," The Man pipes up. He quickly retracts and returns to his positive tone. He has been much more positive as of late.

"All of this is good for you as a writer. The struggle. Your father's near death accident when you were in your early twenties. Your mother's perpetual health issues, her cancer, your cousin's death, your son's Down syndrome, the horrible divorce you lived through, your ex-wife's vendetta against you and your current wife, your own phobias, your bullying boss at work, how it's been difficult to publish your second book after your first. They fuel your growth."

"My growth? Then why do I feel like I am always sinking. And every time I see a little light, I sink deeper into something else? I think it's about time I see someone."

"Do you think that someone will tell you anything different? You are a creator, an artist, you foolish man. That never changes, no matter what drugs they prescribe you, or how much time you spend on a couch. You are obviously depressed, and anxious—all of the trendy words these days. So I won't tell you the obvious, like every other."

"Really?"

"Yes. But I will tell you what will happen as a result of all of these shortcomings?"

"Shortcomings?"

"Yes."

"What?"

"You will experience post-traumatic growth."

"Post-traumatic growth?"

"I assume you don't believe me?"

I know he is trying to be nice. I don't know why, or if he truly feels sorry for me himself, but he has his intentions disguised expertly. I feel he is fooling me now while I am vulnerable.

"Did you make up that term?"

"Of course not. Look it up yourself. It was coined by Richard Tedeschi to describe people who experienced profound changes, major transformations, as they coped with various types of trauma and challenging circumstances, like yourself."

It sounds believable, but I never believe him, so it is hard to taste, swallow and digest.

"When does the growth happen?"

"You poor soul."

"Don't pity me."

"Why not, you're asking for it."

"I'm not asking for it. I don't know how it's happening to me, what is causing it. I may need an objective eye to see me from the outside in. Unlike you, apparently, who has taught himself to see me from the inside out."

"You are eating your lunch alone and enjoying it that way. You used to work a room. Students and teachers would gravitate to you, to your energy, to your passion and intensity and now you prefer to eat alone. You are hiding in the open."

"From what?"

"The truth of who you really are. You are no prince, you are no Hamlet avenging his father. You're just a small town boy from Thorold trying to make himself more important. You starve for importance, don't you? You crave it. You live for it in the same way the janitor at your school pretends to know something more about the stock market. He is always trying to prove he is more important than a janitor. You are always trying to prove you are more important than a teacher. But you are a dime a dozen. I'm sorry to tell you."

His words are true to form and it silences the room more than the absence of people. Even the hum of the fridge from the kitchenette has disappeared.

"What is the post-traumatic growth again?"

"Okay, now we're getting somewhere. Sometimes you have to hit the water below rock bottom first.

"Like I said, all of these circumstances, unfortunate though they may be, will only create a greater appreciation for life, open up new possibilities, improve your relationships, make you more spiritual. Trauma doesn't crush you, according to this theory, it sets the stage for your self-improvement."

"You sound like an extended horoscope. Why do you assume you are my friend?"

"Do you see any others in the room offering you these pearls?"

"That's not very nice."

"People naturally develop and rely on a set of beliefs and assumptions that they've formed about the world, and in order for growth to occur after a trauma, the traumatic event must deeply challenge those beliefs. Trauma shatters worldviews, beliefs and identities like an earthquake—look it up. Even our foundational structures, like the extended family you lean on. Everything crumbles and you will shake, but after everything clears, you will find a desire to rebuild it all over again."

A teacher walks in to interrupt our conversation. He is sniffing around for leftover food or scraps left from the previous lunch. He is hungry. He smiles and moves out of the room.

"Rebuild, Dean. That's what you have already started to do with this new novel. The others have failed, your life has failed you in so many ways, but you are rebuilding, despite your physical inability to walk straight some days, or sleep through a night."

I leave the lunch room and find myself keywording the theory, "post-traumatic growth." It is everything The Man previously explained and more.

"Loss and gain are interrelated," the article explains. "Out of loss, there can be creative gain."

"Adverse events can be so powerful that they force us to think about questions we never would have thought of otherwise."

I return to the empty lunch room but it is empty no longer. The Man is nowhere to be found. In the past, he might have stuck around to remind me that "he told me so." He took great pleasure in proving me wrong, his creator, the writer of his story. But ever since he traumatized the story by taking advantage of Sabal, another character in the story, he seems different, almost mature. Is he growing more, as a character, outside the story? Is that possible without putting him in scenes, testing his greatest weaknesses with conflicts foreign to him? Involving him in relationships with others? Maybe I should write him in some way? But where? Kashif is now driving the story forward. He has taken over first billing and as a result, the landscape of the world I have created is becoming more colourful and suspenseful. The plot is also coming together. Introducing The Man at this juncture might threaten the new fabric of this direction.

Or is his behaviour a ploy to get me to involve him some more? Perhaps his sexual encounter with Sabal, in between the lines, inspired his appetite to exist more. I created him not to have any human qualities like pity, regret, or guilt. I created him as a man who was as close to achieving immortality as a suffering saint or mystic. So why have I kept him on the outside, all of this time? Perhaps I have devalued him and he is insulted as a result of my ignorance.

He isn't in my classroom when I enter my last period of the day. With newfound adrenaline, I deviate from my planned lesson and nearly float on air with an inspired Shakespearean improvisation.

DAY 24

The Messenger can barely see Kashif ahead of him. He has separated himself again, even from Gibran, the goat. The Messenger appreciates the goat's pace. Its brittle limbs barely maintain balance on the side of the road. Every once and a while, The Messenger leads it away from the steep cliff's edge.

A few hours into the walk, Kashif is sitting at the cliff's edge himself, staring out into the mountainous distance.

"Why did you stop?"

"This is where we are going."

He points over the valley of green.

"We will climb that mountain?"

"Will Gibran be able to handle it? The walk down is steep."

"You distrust his abilities."

Kashif slides down a little before leaning back to walk down the cliff from the road and not fall over. The Messenger focuses on Gibran. He tries to get the goat to go first, but the animal refuses him. Kashif has already disappeared into the bush.

"Okay, if you don't want to come, stay here."

The Messenger begins his descent and uses his hands on the rocks to support himself. When he reaches the flatter valley below, Kashif is far ahead of him while Gibran is lost behind him. Until he hears steps.

The goat is tiptoeing its way down. The baggage it is carrying is pressing forward on its head, but the goat is resilient. It extends its neck backward. It is obedient. It knows its job. To lose the bag is more perilous than tumbling down the cliff. Not worried anymore, The Messenger looks ahead. He hears the crunching of branches and follows the echo of the sound.

The goat reaches level ground unscathed, fully balanced. It yelps a little as if to cheer before following the trail by sound himself. It appears like a long time before The Messenger finds Kashif in a slight clearing before the incline of the mountain. He is sharpening a branch. His strokes are long and straight. The branch bends into the knife with appreciative slivers flailing onto the ground.

"Have a seat. Rest a little before we take the mountain."

The Messenger prefers to lean against a tree. The falling pine needles of the cedar make a sparkling sound up above.

"Have you thought of a story to sell me with yet?"

Kashif continues to shave the branch and The Messenger wonders if he will shave it entirely into nothing. It is almost nothing, its width the size of a finger.

"You have been away for fifteen years. You were captured, and then escaped?"

"Who captured me?"

"Another group?"

"Impossible."

"Why?"

"No group can claim responsibility for such an act. Terror is all about responsibility. That is the selling point."

"You disappeared to another country?"

"Also impossible. They have been looking for me. Even those who believed me dead. Your story must be good enough to eliminate my martyr status. The story must be very believable."

"What really happened? How did you martyr yourself?"

"I created a death scene."

"Why?"

"Because I couldn't live the same anymore."

"Why not?"

"I found out about her."

"Your daughter? That's understandable."

"I didn't know she existed. For five years, I didn't know she existed. And then I woke up one day knowing a part of me was dying somewhere. It was something I never felt before. Something within me separated itself from the whole. I don't know how to describe it, really."

"So you knew she existed even before you really knew she existed."

"Yes." He stops talking and shaving the stick now that Gibran is made visible in the bush. Gibran's whiteness is almost unicorn-like in the brush.

"Her mother never told me. She never wanted to tell me. She never wanted her to know. So I went in search of her, one day. To do so, I created my death scene. I staged a death scene and then left blood in my place. My blood. On a mountain like this. I took pictures and sent them to the television network. They created the rest of the story. They had my blood to prove it was me, but not a body. That's how you create a martyr. You remove the body from the scene. It always leaves a tiny space of doubt to fuel the legend."

"What did they determine the cause of death to be?"

"The explanations varied. From foreign enemies, to suicide, to Mohammed taking me as a prophet from the mountain as a sacrifice. This one usurped the rest."

"How did you find her?"

"I ventured into every hospital on the planet, and I followed my instincts."

"How long did it take you to find her?"

"Five years. I found her in a nunnery. Abandoned by her mother."

"Do you know her mother?"

"I know she is mine."

"How?"

"I took her blood. Blood will have blood, isn't that what they say."

Gibran is proud to have reached the cleared out space in the forest. The goat is breathing heavy, but Kashif, in a swift move, inserts the threadlike sharpened branch into the goat's chest and the goat instantly keels over. The Messenger is shocked by how quickly it happens. Gibran's eyes are wide open, as if never seeing it coming.

"Why did you do that?"

"I don't know. I felt you were as hungry as I am."

Kashif removes the baggage from the goat's back and delicately lifts the goat onto his shoulder.

"Take the bag, will you?"

They leave the spot without a story. The Messenger follows Kashif and is able to keep up with him as he climbs up the mountain. The goat's mouth is dripping blood and creating a trail for other predators to sniff out.

When they reach an area before the zenith of the mountain, Kashif walks into a cave reserved from a primitive history. This is a hiding shelter he has used before, The Messenger believes. Kashif leaves a limp Gibran on the sand in front of the cave before he enters. When he returns, and like he has seen a God, he is bearded again, as he was for the picture.

"It is time to get back into character."

"Why did you kill Gibran?"

"We have to eat, before we are kidnapped. It will be like a last supper."

Kashif removes a long, sheathing blade from his tunic. He begins skinning the goat.

"Can you prepare a fire?"

The Messenger does as he is told. He collects branches and twigs and kindle. He then finds a split tree, deadened on the slope. He procures a thicker piece of wood to weight the rest of it down. It takes him a while to light the fire, but he does so expertly. It doesn't impress Kashif in the least. He is busy skinning the goat. When he breaks its limbs, The Messenger shivers. As if synchronized, the fire bursts into a taller flame when Kashif, hands bloodied and steaming with the goat's warmth, carries the blanket of goat parts to the fire. He washes his hands cleanly and then he sharpens some more twigs with his knife. The Messenger wonders if he is sharpening the branches for him, this time around, but he is making skewers. He offers a few to The Messenger.

"So what will be believable as my story," Kashif asks, as if teasing The Messenger. He seems to already have the story stored in his mind. This is a test, The Messenger considers. If he passes it, Kashif will regard him as someone worthy to represent his public interests.

"I need to know one thing more."

"What is that?"

The meat on the stick is bubbling away its water in the translucence of the flame.

"Who was her mother?"

"There were many women. I told you, I don't know."

"As you said, I need to know the truth before I can create a believable fiction."

Kashif smirks.

"She was a daughter herself. Of one of our funders. You will meet him when we are captured, I am sure. It's the reason I didn't want to tell you the entire truth. I didn't want it to show on your face."

"He doesn't know."

"I met her here, in Lebanon first, and then she hunted me in the African desert. She was a privileged girl, but too curious. Her father had sent her away to learn languages and other cultures. She had disguised herself."

"She found you?"

"Yes, she is the only one to find me. Aside from you."

"How did she know who you were?"

"Well, first she came to understand her father's secrets. He is a powerful man, but she was a resourceful girl. And then, after the discovery of her father's power, she chased its most dangerous weapon."

"Before you had changed?"

"I am always changing."

"Before your surgeries, I mean."

"Yes. My reputation as a chameleon is believed to be ingenious, and many concur I am completely devoted to the craft of terror. The real reason for these changes was to hide myself from her, not from those who placed bounties on my head."

"Why would you want to hide yourself from her—her father?"

"Her father knows nothing of anything. These are secrets I will keep beyond the afterlife."

The Messenger waits without asking. He understands this is the best way to achieve the truth from someone in a mountainside confessional. Silence is the most appropriate lure and the campfire provides the perfect warmth for trust.

"She made me human. It is that simple. I was created immortal in my instincts, but she made me human."

Kashif offers the first cooked piece to The Messenger and he is appreciative. Even without spice or salt, it is pleasing to the taste. There is blood in the aftertaste.

"You cannot survive as long as I have with weakness. In this world, weakness is only employed as a trap. She weakened me and I worried it would endanger her. My own weakness. One day, she sent me a picture of herself in a hospital bed. She knew where I was hiding all along. She died, and our daughter was dying of the same disease, but she wouldn't tell me. So I disappeared to find her and I have never reappeared since."

"How did she know where to find you?"

"She had her ways. I never questioned her as the mother of my daughter. My daughter is not like her mother—my daughter refuses to die. She refutes peace, like her father. I never make myself recognizable to her. I dress as random visitors but I believe she knows it is me, just like her mother knew how to find me."

"By instinct?"

"Very funny. So what is the story?"

"I thought about it the whole walk here. There are private stories and there are stories meant for public consumption."

Kashif leans in and his chin seems to rest on the tip of a fluttering flame.

"If you say you have come out of hiding, your audience will question your cowardice. They will consider you broken, mentally, or by nerves."

"I agree. I agree."

The Messenger is somewhat surprised Kashif is listening to him so intently. Why does he want him to make up the story?

"Why did you stop?"

"Sorry. A thought crossed my mind."

"You are wondering why I am entrusting you with my story."

"How do you do that?"

"What?"

"Guess so accurately."

"I have been living my life by the same feeling, the same hunches, and the same instincts. It's a language all to its own. But to answer your question, I need your objectivity. It is the reason you are alive right now. A story coming directly from me will carry a dangerous bias, like I am making it up. Like it is contrived for an ulterior motive. However, if you tell my story, you will gain the credit of having found me and that credibility will serve the story better. Your story will be from a distance, getting closer and closer the more you tell it. This will inspire those who have been searching for me for fifteen years, to find us."

"Which is why, I believe, we should take the religious route with your story. If you claim mystical status, like a saint or a prophet called, or even an angel, for that matter, your audience will fear your absence, they will grow curious to the unknown, and they will listen to everything you have to say without question."

Kashif smirks and the fire lends it more width with a lined shadow on his face, from ear to ear.

"We will present you as a monk called to a religious rite of passage. You were called to Mecca; you were called by the prophet Mohammed. You have returned to pave a new wave of terror. One that will revolutionize the term."

"This will explain my absence."

"This will also introduce you to the child who can save your daughter. Your resurrection will explain why he exists. A prophet paving the road for a second coming."

"You stole that from another religion."

"Is that what a story is in the first place? Something stolen from another's perspective?"

Kashif slaps his lap before taking a big bite of meat from a stick charred by the fire. The Messenger wonders if it is burning his tongue.

"This is why you are alive. I knew not to kill you, even though I should have. I could feel I needed you. We must dramatize and record this story. It must be brief in its first installment, in the firelight. We will build this story and they will come to find us on the mountain."

Kashif disappears into the cave to retrieve his bag. He removes a brand new, traceable phone and it lights up his face once he turns the power on.

"It's time for us to move now."

DAY 26

Kashif positions himself at a defined angle to the fire. Half of him is behind the fire, the other half revealed by it. One side of his bearded face is in the orange fire light and the other erased by the black in the dark.

"When you are ready, ask the questions. Be sure to cut off the answer of the second, the way we rehearsed it."

The fire pops a sparkle into the night. It floats away until it extinguishes and disappears. The Messenger presses the red record button on the phone.

"Why have you returned?"

"I was sent back by The Prophet. I was dead, now I am alive again."

"What is your mission?"

"To create a new jihad. To renew the old with the new. To pave the way for—"

The Messenger presses the button. Kashif asks him to replay it. The take is a good one. Kashif is convinced by it.

"Perfect, you can see the old cedars in the corner of the screen. They will know how to find us now."

"Do you want to try it again?"

"No, send it."

The Messenger sends it to the email Kashif spells out to him. They listen to the sound of the message sending before the air is silenced again by the glow of the phone, by the glow of the fire, by the smoggy scent of burning flesh.

"Now we wait, and watch."

"What are we watching for?" asks The Messenger.

"The battle before the victory. After the victory, we will be delivered to the council. The victor will lead us to the child. You can sleep, if you wish. You must be very tired. I will stand watch."

The Messenger is tired and his head is spinning for some reason. The orientation of the mountain against a darkening sky creates a vibrating effect. Or perhaps it was something he ate, or the guilt from having eaten an animal he had grown close to in so short a time.

He passes out before he can fall asleep thinking. He dreams of Gibran, the goat, numerous times. In each series of dreams the goat is mutated. In one of them, the goat's head replaces Kashif's on his body. Kashif is the goat, eating himself in another.

An explosion awakens him instantly. It is the crack of dawn and Kashif is statue-like in the same place. His hands on his knees, his eyes are focussed on a trail of smoke rising from the valley.

I stop writing because I am forcing words out of my fingers. Each sentence feels like I am stretching it off the page. I find myself reverting back to rewrite paragraphs that require essential plot details or descriptions. I fear I am questioning the validity of the entire story too much at this point, now that I see its end approaching. The story wants to funnel quickly to its resolution point and I am resisting the swirling vortex of the flush. It is begging to be finished but I am trying to slow it down. I want to apply the same intensity and attention to detail in the last pages as I had in the first. I don't want it to end, as well. For personal reasons. This is my metaphorical getaway for life's more serious issues. This is my total escape. Mind, Body, Spirit. This story has become the only work that energizes me in this trinity.

I would like to blame my day job teaching as continuing to disappoint me but I can't scapegoat my career. It has been good to me over the years. It has helped me come out of my shell. It has given me purpose, acclaim, appreciation, and inspiration, with further room for future fulfilment. And yet I feel myself failing it with my insatiable dreams.

By this point in my life I assumed I would be writing full time. Transitioning from my public career into a private one. Living off of my books, and not by the protocol of a rigid routine. Establishing a name for myself in the industry. I have fallen short of my aspirations, fallen shorter and older by all accounts and expectations. I haven't been able to put together another novel worthy of publication and the possibility of writing for a living has become a pipe dream someone else is smoking the life out of.

I want to talk to my wife about it. I hear the roll of the tread-mill downstairs and I know she is exercising. The kids are asleep. The rest of the house is dark.

I find her with her headphones on. She is running at an impressive speed. When she sees me, she removes them and slows the pace down.

"Hey."

"I was thinking, I would like to build that cottage up north. Maybe we should go modular home instead."

"Why did we spend money on architectural plans then?"

She seems disgusted by my suggestion. Her voice is nearly hateful and everything in it is rejection.

In a predictable act of desperately grasping for one last hope, I purchased a waterfront lot on a small lake in Muskoka a year back. It was supposed to be a place my family could retreat to since there are six of us, and one with an inability to walk on and off a plane for a normal vacation destination. Deep down it was also to be my writing retreat, and we were supposed to build a dream cottage, rent it out and pay off the mortgage that way, while enjoying the offseason weekends. I purchased it on a line of credit. My wife agreed because she believed it would be a family investment, one that our Down syndrome child would familiarize good times in. The idea seemed golden until both of my brothers invested in local commercial properties that yielded better monetary returns. Both of them are more successful than me and I am very proud of them. I don't spite their success or good decisions. I can tell my wife sees our investment in a differ-ent, comparative light now.

I try my best to explain. To salvage the initial dream, when it appeared like such a good idea.

"It may be too expensive to build the architectural way."

"You know what, this is irrelevant right now. Why are you bringing it up to me?"

"Because I've been getting some quotes and I wanted to start slowly."

"We can't start! We will never be able to start! We have no money to start it!"

I can see lost faith in her eyes, in my presumed talent, in what she thought I was when she married me.

"I just thought."

"You don't think like a businessman because you are a shitty businessman."

I know where this is coming from. I don't know it all just yet. My mind is critically thinking ahead of itself, analyzing every implicit meaning.

We are arguing about a dream. Or I am arguing about a dream because she is not refuting the dream. Instead she is attacking my lack of attention in her life since we received the news of her escape from cancer. When I am writing long hours before and after work, I become quiet and aloof in between. I don't ask questions. I don't take interest in or remember important family events I should share in as a husband and father. I am consumed by the words I write to the point where they consume the goodness in my life. They bring light to my eyes, but darkness everywhere else. So I can see why the cottage is a bad idea at this point in time. It represents another distraction from them.

I don't see this angle right away. It hurts me right away when she insults me, so much so that I begin to leave before turning around for more.

"Like you're a good businessman? What have you done to push us forward?"

Neither of us is arguing about business anymore. Our tones are violent, our words sharper still. Although we breach topics like the cottage, my inability to make the same money as my brothers or our bad luck with investments, there is only one reason why we fight.

"I don't want to be in the same room with you anymore. I don't want to see you. I don't want to be here. I'm leaving."

"Then go," I answer. "I don't care anymore."

We both seek escape. We both want to run, a new race, on a new track, with a real victory at the end. Not a consolation victory. Not a moral victory. A victory that doesn't come with the constant acceptance of loss, one set apart from changing a five-year-old's diapers, or trying to force Tobias to eat something more than cookies and bread with peanut butter. We are frustrated with the daily toil of parents dealing with the slow progress of a disability. And what kills us more is that we would never trade him for anyone else. It's the love we have for him that is the killer. It is the love that we bear him that carves new entry points of pessimism and comparison with everyone outside of our own struggles. Even our families don't understand, and why should they want to understand how difficult it is to confront the same reality day in and day out, knowing full well it could only get a little better if it's a good day.

I hate my wife as I scream at her. And I know she hates me. Her words, her voice, the way her arms move to clear the air I breathe, all point to someone, anyone, to blame. How else can you be alive to understand acceptance, true acceptance with no doorway to change, without anyone to blame?

So we blame each other and begin to destroy what's left of us.

The good. All that is good. Oh, how we take for granted all that is good between us.

I retreat to my office again but not to write. I don't want The Man to see me in this defeated state. No creator should be seen in such a context. Creators are omniscient. Creators are all knowing. Creators are not shitty businessmen.

Instead, I search for properties in cottage country. I escape into their views, onto their docks, in their forested landscapes nestled privately in a green bush, while I hear her packing a bag. I walk out of the office.

"You're not going anywhere."

"I can't stay here. I'm going to a hotel. You don't know how it is. You go to work, you don't see it all. You can make yourself numb for a few hours before they go to bed, but you don't know. You never know. You never want to know."

She is stuffing clothes from the laundry basket into one of the kid's knapsacks. I know she isn't going anywhere because she hasn't changed out of her pajamas.

"I don't want you to go. Sleep upstairs, I'll sleep downstairs."

"You can't run and think it won't be here when you come back."

This is the point when I realize why she is really upset with me. It convinces her temporarily.

Dejected, she takes the laundry basket up to our bedroom. The light goes off and it gets colder in the darkened home without her.

DAY 27

"They are here."

The Messenger wakes with a dry mouth and the taste of rotten flesh in his mouth. Kashif hasn't moved an inch from his position last night. He doesn't appear tired. He doesn't yawn or rub his eyes. The height of the fire has lessened and he is staring over it with an intense look. The Messenger follows the direction of his eye line to hear noises in the battle. No voices. The trees twitch violently. Every once in a while there is a groan, or a moan. The noises and the rustling of trees gets closer and closer like a wave of energy, like an invisible harmattan gaining momentum as it swallows more air and condensation.

"Are you ready to go yet?" Kashif asks.

"You know where we are going?"

"Whoever reaches the mountain alive will take us towards the Syrian border. There will be a few sabotage attacks before we reach it. After we cross the border, there will be another battle, after which we will be transferred. When we reach our final destination, there will be an economic war, or negotiation, and the victor will present us to the council to achieve ranking."

"Ranking?"

"Yes. All of the groups are ranked. Capturing me is a coup. The story we made up will keep us alive the whole journey."

The Messenger finds a seat next to Kashif, not too close. The space around him appears electric, like an invisible fence.

Screams now disrupt the forest as dawn spreads itself against the valley with a thinning mist. The Messenger can hear the language of battle now. It is directional, instructive. Kashif doesn't move or flinch. He is planted in his spot and his eyes close, not to rest or meditate. He is definitely listening to something within him, a selection of music.

The violence is now ascending the mountain and bullet sounds are heard splicing into missed targets. Trees, rock-embedded ground, ricocheting off of cliffs. Grenade explosions shake the mountain a little. The slicing of missed arrows cuts the air. The Messenger's stomach is disturbed. He doesn't know if it is indigestion or Gibran awakening within him, fearing the outcome of this battle.

"Are we to sit still?"

Kashif doesn't hear him. He is locked now in his trancelike state.

The Messenger can hear voices getting closer. And then it becomes quiet. Peaceful.

Three men emerge onto the scene. They slowly approach, place their guns on the ground gently, so as not to awake Kashif. And then they crouch their way to the fire. They pay no attention to The Messenger. By the time they reach the area by the fire, they are crawling on their knees. The Messenger can determine they are similarly in a trance. Their eyes are widened and softened now. There is blood on their attire, on their faces. Their eyes are captive to the vision before them. When Kashif opens his eyes fully, they place their cheeks to the ground. Although they are bearded themselves, one with his entire face nearly rolling in waves of hair, they are scrawny and young.

They don't speak. They transform into attentive students, stopping a respectable distance away not to encroach upon the hallowed ground of their teacher.

Kashif observes them as if to recognize a signature. After acquiring a positive identification, he assumes the role. He rises gently, as if in slow motion. His movements now have transformed. No longer are they determined and forceful. Now they are languid and fluid, like a dancer's. His face transforms in synchronicity to his movements. He appears as an elder now, a rabbi breaming with wisdom.

The changes are different, this time around, or so The Messenger observes. These changes are not base level contortions or facial manipulations. This transformation is transcendent. Method acting. Kashif's body is obeying what he believes himself to be right now—a spiritual leader. Even his fingers appear different. No longer wire-like with a strong grip around a scaling knife, they are softened and the skin on the edges of the knuckles is softer, wrinkled.

"I have returned," he speaks in an assuring whisper now. His voice is raspier. He has become the story they put together the night before. He has become the man who has seen a god. His body believes it. He makes his body believe it somehow and the fiction becomes truth before The Messenger's eyes.

"Let us assume the honour of delivering you to our Masters. They will be pleased to welcome you."

One of the boys rushes into the cave as if knowing there is baggage within. How would he know, The Messenger questions. Is Kashif communicating telepathically with them, or is it his body language dictating the details of their obedience?

The young boy returns from the cave with the baggage. Everyone's attention shifts towards The Messenger. Their eyes are appreciative to him, even Kashif's. The boy with the blanketing face beard offers him a hand to help The Messenger from the ground. The Messenger takes it.

"Thank you for finding him."

Through the beard, The Messenger detects a good boy, someone who listens to his father.

They lead the way down the mountain and into the valley. Along the path dotted by Gibran's blood, there are mutilated bodies, a series of battle casualties. All of the men are young and barely out of boyhood. The Messenger tries to get Kashif's attention but he is too focussed now. He floats behind his escorts, while they constantly look back to see if he is real. The bearded boy walks behind The Messenger to protect them from a back door attack.

When The Messenger glances behind him, he sees the smoke rise from the fire he created the night before. No one motioned to put it out for fear of disrupting its dying energy.

Day 28

"I see what you're trying to do. You're trying to make him a hero."

"I am doing no such thing. I am simply creating him at this stage in his life," I explain to The Man. He is stalking me on my midnight walks. It is cold and wintery outside and this is another attempt to gain an uninterrupted night of sleep. I like the silence when everyone else is asleep. And I feel better the next morning, no matter how many hours I sleep.

"He has too many sins to account for. He can never be a true hero, even if he manages to save his daughter's life. It doesn't exonerate him from everyone he has killed, or those who have died because of him. Even Macbeth as a serial killer pales in comparison."

I should have known The Man would find me, even in my attempts to sneak away from life in the middle of the night. He has a nose for privacy and whenever he catches a scent he invades and attacks my peace.

"He is only doing what his instincts are dictating to him right now."

"Don't get me wrong, Dean. I do like his makeup. Not your stereotypical terrorist or former terrorist. He is creative, not brainwashed, but organic, one in line with his surroundings despite his ability to change like a chameleon in plain sight. By the way, is this what you will title the work—Chameleon?"

"I was thinking more along the lines of Karma Chameleon, like the Boy George song."

"Now you're just being silly."

"Are you jealous?"

"Of whom?"

"Of the way I created him above you."

"I haven't even developed yet. I admit, I like his creativity, his superpower ability to transform. That's a nice touch. But this isn't a superhero story, Dean. This is supposed to be a literary novel. I thought you were aiming for the fences with this one. You were so angry in the preface. It was like you were fed up with everything and you had a chip on your shoulder. And from that beautiful anger, I emerged. This guy seems a little too soft for his history."

"And you know his history?"

"If you are basing him partially on the real chameleon, the Hezbollah leader of the eighties, yes, I am familiar with that history. You created me to be investigative and wise above my means. I suppose he is a character foil of me, a sexier version? Kashif is an artist. He commands attention by his talents and his innate, natural abilities. I can see why you would want him as your protagonist, even above The Messenger, who, to me, is the unsung hero of this novel thus far. Listen up though, you can't make someone who isn't heroic into a hero. It will never fly."

"Why not?"

I can almost see the words from my mouth forming in my visible breath. My heartbeat is accelerating because I am walking faster subconsciously. My feet want to get away from The Man without realizing he doesn't have real feet. Fictional feet are always faster.

"Because as a character you emerge from your context and his context is evil, not good."

"What context did you emerge from?" I ask him.

"The brink of you quitting as a writer."

I've thought about it and I know The Man is alluding to this consideration. I know I am a writer. I am sensitive to everything I see, touch, feel, hear and encounter. I am too observant to the point of distraction. I love to read until my eyes burn and my whole being comes alive when I am engaged in a story. But sometimes, this isn't enough. There are many artists who fall unrequited. There are many creators who are rejected by a chameleon-like world.

When I first fell in love with writing, I decided I would write a novel. I was eighteen and it ended up being a novella. I found an ad for a literary agency in Pittsburgh. I sent them my novella and they returned a letter asking me to send the entire manuscript. They also quoted me an "editing" charge. That whole first semester of university, I worked on extending the novella into a full-length novel. I stalled the agency and when it was time, I sent the whole book and a cheque from my savings for this editing fee. It returned edited all right, and also with a contract for representation.

I remember feeling so happy, so accomplished, so hopeful. This is what I wanted to do. This is how I wanted to live my life, creating stories along the way. I felt confident and better than the students in my seminar sections who were too focussed on impressing the professor with big words. They would discuss my stories one day, I resolved under my breath.

Three months later, I received a letter stating that a publishing company wanted to publish my novel. The exhilaration was unbearable. I told all of my friends and family. Everyone was so proud. I felt important to them, and most importantly, to myself. The condition for publication required another cheque, which my parents without question provided as a gift.

Eight months later I was told the publisher had gone bankrupt. Two weeks after that I received a notice from a lawyer with a number of other writers swindled into giving money to both the agency and the publisher.

I had been duped, humiliated. I would have to tell everyone who was special to me that the book wasn't going to come out, that I had been scammed, that I wasn't as talented as they thought.

The rejection and dejection initiated me. It introduced me to real sorrow, true embarrassment, and it might have broken a window on the house of my academic security.

So I started to look into M.A. programs. I was going to learn the craft from the ground up. Start publishing short stories and poems in literary journals like all of my favourite authors, whose bios I had scavenged to find similar rejections.

I attended writing retreats, went to Harbourfront to listen to some authors. When I reached the front of the line to have Rohinton Mistry sign my *Fine Balance* novel, I was bursting again with the question.

"Did you ever encounter rejection as a writer?"

"Rejection? No, no, I was never rejected."

I wanted to kill him but there were too many gawking witnesses who gazed upon him like a god of literature.

I think about the very beginning on my walk and I presume The Man is listening to my thoughts. I am exposing myself to him. This, I know, is dangerous. I don't like him studying me. There should be limitations to his understanding of his creator. Some mystery. Otherwise, he will not act like the character I created him to be.

"You made me a mystery," he says softly, almost regretfully.

"I'm sorry."

"You didn't think me worthy enough to be a hero? Was I solely the prologue guy who comes out on stage first to quiet down the crowd before the play starts?"

These are his words, I know, but they are my thoughts. Does that make sense? He speaks what I truly think of him and ironically, when he says the words, he comes across as hurt.

"I spend so much time with you that I never think to insert you in the story," I say to The Man.

"Which is why I inserted myself into it earlier."

"I don't want you to do that anymore."

"I promise."

"Sometimes you create someone and the story dictates the direction of his life. I created you and him the same way. I thought about you both. I got to know you both. I researched you both. I crafted you with everything I was capable of. But the story takes on a life of its own, just like life happening when you don't go to work, or when you don't leave the house. Does that make sense?"

"Perfect sense. If the story needs me, it will find me." The Man is satisfied.

"Exactly."

We walk in the boundaries of this conversation around the neighbourhood. Most of the lights are out, this time of night. There are a few burning in upper windows or flickering from a screen in another. Every time I consider turning back, I decide to change my direction. This sudden turn lengthens the walk and usually includes another couple of blocks. It is so quiet I can hear the sound of trucks on the highway. What a lonely life it must be to drive without passengers at this hour. I can only imagine how many voices a driver must hear on his way to nowhere in particular.

DAY 29

Kashif follows the boys through the foliage but slows his pace as he does so. He is trying to gain space from them, The Messenger believes, just as he did from him on their walk to the mountain. The Messenger wonders if there is something wrong. He is not speeding up as he did on the way to the mountain. In this scene, he is separating himself in reverse, which confuses the young bearded man covering the backside.

"Do you need some water?" The young man scrambles through his shoulder sack. The others stop once they notice.

"Keep walking," Kashif advises them. They obey.

Kashif takes the water canteen and pushes the bearded boy back a few steps. In one motion, he pulls The Messenger close to him.

An arrow lodges itself in the young boy's chest. Minutes later, the two leading the way are ambushed with machetes. The thump of the weapons gouging flesh is a familiar sound to The Messenger, as are the moans before death. It reminds him of the time he was stabbed by the doctor who saved him.

From the thickened brush ahead of them a new group emerges, while the one lodged in the tree, who shot the arrow, climbs down. The Messenger is impressed by Kashif's ability to sense danger and protect himself with space. The space has now become his territory, and once again, this new group of terror soldiers hesitate to approach him.

"We have come to bring you to them."

The Messenger stands closer to Kashif. The closer he stands to him, the more protected he feels. He doesn't understand why he no longer wishes to die. Before having met Kashif or Sabal, he would have welcomed any opportunity, like this one, to be killed. Now he fears death again. Has Kashif created this fear in him? Has Kashif introduced him to another level of fear, the one without a cure?

He had read many books about death addicts. Those who couldn't stop thinking of the final act, those who craved it every moment of the day. He considered these people kindred spirits of his. He had read that Therese Lisieux, the child saint, actually became disappointed when her God made her wait. She died young, but not young enough to her. She craved dying like she craved food to survive.

These men, these new soldiers, are also young, or so The Messenger observes, although slightly older than the last troop. They appear more rugged in their skin texture. Foreigners to this land. Their heads are square and unclothed.

Kashif refuses to speak aloud. He only speaks when necessary.

The leader of this troop of five venerates him with a humble bow. They treat Kashif like royalty, revere him as they would heroes read about before bedtime as children. Another man unclasps a box on his belt. He unburies a tiny perfume bottle and pours it on Kashif's sandaled feet.

"It has been blessed," he explains.

Kashif nods and peers in the direction he wants them to walk towards. They understand the instruction.

The Messenger follows cognizant of the fact these men leading them will also perish before their final destination.

DAY 30

This troop is much more foolish. They take pictures with their phones and it is obvious they are seeking fame from the capture. Kashif is stoic to the flashes. He walks within their shadows and slows his pace again. There is no one guarding the backside this time, so he waits while they move ahead enough not to hear him whisper under his lips.

"Are you thirsty?"

"Yes."

Kashif slips The Messenger the canteen. The water is surprisingly cold.

"Have you ever killed another man?"

"No."

"This is the reason you can't kill yourself. Do you want to die, still?"

"How do you know I am rethinking it?"

"Your face is different. You found some peace watching the others die. You reacted more when I killed the goat. You are growing insensitive to death. Death doesn't come to the sensitive, just the unsuspecting."

The Messenger had never thought of it this way. Kashif makes it sound so formulaic, almost scientific.

"I have killed too many. And too many have been killed because of me. These boys live only for the moment. They don't know what evil has befallen them."

The Messenger believes Kashif knows their own final destination, even where the miracle child is held captive.

"Do you know where the boy is?"

Kashif doesn't say a word.

"If you do, why don't we go and find him ourselves. No one else needs to die. This is the worst escort service ever."

"You're right. It is necessary. For the boy to leave with us, these are the sacrifices."

"You have a plan, I'm assuming."

"It is already in motion."

"How will it end?"

"It will end at the hospital. I will save her for good."

In between these snippets of conversation, The Messenger analyzes the value of one life over another. He had always believed that the value of one could never exceed the same. What made one life more important or less expensive in the yin yang of supply and demand? And how could one life usurp the importance of another? Was there a balance at stake? Did catastrophes arise as a result of an imbalance? To even the score, or to adjust the values?

Kashif acts like the young lives ending tragically before him, literally at his feet, are worth less than his daughter's life, worth less than his own. He acts like an immortal entrapped in a human form and this arrogance annoys The Messenger.

"What if I decide to leave you now?"

"Someone will kill you."

"Will you kill me?"

"I am keeping you alive."

"I wanted to die."

"You will, like all of us, in the proper time of your destiny."

His words make too much sense, thinks The Messenger, which makes them despicable to listen to. The young boys ahead of them, their machine guns at their sides, are eating ravenously, like famished children. The Messenger catches the scent of ripened fruit while shards of peel float upon the longer grass on either side of them.

"Stop," Kashif advises.

An explosion is set off and the boys are vaulted to an area twenty feet behind them.

"Don't look back. Don't ever look back," Kashif raises his voice.

The sound of a vehicle intrudes upon the smoke rising from the detonated explosion site.

"We will move forward now."

Kashif walks into the smoke. He is swallowed by a wall of trees and the invisible sound of an engine.

When I was younger, I remember my father taking me out to drive for the first time. I think I was thirteen or so and he was bored. Or just waiting for his friends to arrive at the coffee shop from a construction site or something. My father, when he walked, worked twelve hour days. He arrived home without a tongue, showered, sat at the head of the table with his shirt off, his skin beading in sweat, his hair perfectly styled and sprayed with chemical.

He ate voraciously and we knew not to bother him. Sometimes, he intimidated us into starting an argument, or forced one of us to outwit him and make him laugh. Then he would leave, midstream, my mother not having eaten yet, dress in his finest clothes and shoes and head to the coffee shop. My mother called it stress relief for building a business. We never called it anything. We were so used to him leaving us.

But that one sunny, spring day, he saw me kicking the ball against the porch steps and he must have felt sorry for me. Fully dressed and emanating cologne, he didn't want to join me playing. I have a fond memory of the first time he volunteered to play with me. I begged him to go in net, between the shrubs in our front yard. He was dressed again in his silk shirt and leather boots. I wanted to prove to him I could score on an adult. I wanted to prove to him I was a good soccer player. I shot the ball towards a corner and it went in but not before dirtying his pants. As he dusted off the mark, he accused me of not aiming for the corner. He lit a cigarette and left right afterwards.

So when he asked me if I wanted to drive for the first time, I didn't know what to say. I was afraid. It meant he was interested in spending time with me so I didn't want to give it up. He threw me the keys and lit his cigarette.

I hopped in the car.

"Where are we going?"

"Don't worry where we are going. Just drive."

I struggled to find my seatbelt.

"What are you doing?" he raised his voice.

"Trying to get the seatbelt to click."

"You don't need the seatbelt. Let's go. Put it in reverse."

I did as I was told. I was so afraid to disappoint him.

"Keep it steady in the middle," he barked out orders. He seemed more upset that I was disrupting the flow his smoking routine, which he always enjoyed while driving himself.

I noticed people in the neighbourhood waving at me but I wouldn't wave back. I kept my eyes on the road and I was obsessed with checking my rearview mirror.

"Get your foot off the brake," he ordered before changing the instruction. "What foot are you using on the brake?"

"My right?"

"And which one on the gas?"

"The same one."

"No,no,no. Put your right foot on the gas and your left foot on the brake. Like a race car driver."

I did as I was told. Years later my driving instructor would nearly kill me for these bad habits, but this was my father, the best driver I had known at the time.

We stopped at a four-way stop and I checked my rearview mirror again.

"What are you doing?"

"Checking behind me. This guy is close."

"Never look behind you. Always look ahead. If you look behind, he will crash into you. People who look behind crash into those who move forward. That's life," he added, and released smoke from his nose. For some reason, I am remembering this scene more and more in my life these days, and I feel foolish for not taking the best advice my father ever gave me.

When I visit him now, I am surprised by the fact he would rather spend time somewhere else. He is trapped in his wheelchair and some days, although it is suffering for him and my mother who nurses him, I believe it to be a blessing in disguise. I never knew my father when he walked, when he worked, when he came home, before. He never talked. We never conversed. And as the first born, he made me the example for the others. After his accident, the wheelchair trapped him into staying in one place, or within arm's length. And I knew my brothers felt the same. Although it was a traumatic experience in all of our lives, the shepherd being struck down and the sheep scattering, we all knew this was our chance to gain his attention, his real attention. I think we spoke more to him while he rested in his coma. And when he woke, and we waited for him to recover, we spoke more to each other in his presence.

He needed us to visit. He needed us to speak to him. He had never been in a hospital before. He had never been sick. To see us visit pleased him. When he returned home, it became a chore for him to talk. It depressed him not to have the freedom of his legs. As much as he tried, I think we came to understand that in his heart we were always the first option, but for his time we could never achieve that status.

Ironically, and not surprisingly, I value my work in the same manner, except for the fact that I enjoy my family and my kids. Perhaps I fear losing them more. Or maybe I have more of my mother in me than my father.

So I finish this session creeping in the dark to hear my children sleep. They breathe so beautifully in the night. I sit on the floor and come to realize that even The Man can't disrupt the peace here.

DAY 31

Kashif and The Messenger have been placed in the back of a dark cargo truck for purposes of discretion before crossing the border. The Messenger can't see Kashif in the dark, which makes him more accessible for conversation.

"Who are these people?" The Messenger asks.

"Another local group. They will serve the purpose of getting us across the border. We will most likely be kidnapped again afterwards."

"How many groups are there?"

"As many as you can imagine. There is a pot of gold at the end of this rainbow, and it is bottomless to whoever brings me in."

"Tell me about her?"

"My daughter?"

"The mother of your daughter."

"Why? She has passed."

Kashif always speaks in a matter of fact manner. There are no emotional links. Just connectors or patterns, with no weight or bias attached to each.

"Did you love her?"

"I don't believe in the term."

"But you love your daughter."

"I ache for her. It's all I know. She suffers and I suffer at the same time."

"I think people call that love."

"I call it pain. And pain needs to be fulfilled. That's all it needs, the fulfilment of release."

"So you are saving her for you?"

"I don't want her to know pain as well as I do."

"She has been suffering a long time. She probably knows it more than you."

"When she is cured, she will live a beautiful life free of it. She will live by the right instincts, and even the wrong ones will guide her to live fully."

"And what about your pain?"

"I am cursed with it. It will never go away."

It is silent in the truck and the ground underneath is one cratered pothole after another. The back cabin shakes and its metal bearings vibrate against the wind.

Kashif confesses.

"I met her at the market. I was tired of my hiding, tired of the people surrounding me for my protection. Tired of their body scents, their jokes, and their feigned sacrificial gestures. So I escaped them to find open air. Not too far away from here. Further north, in the mountains. A festival for a village Saint. I could hear children's voices and ripened fruit luring me to the center of the village. No one recognized me. They paid me no attention at all, really. They focused on the statue of the bearded saint in a procession up another mountain. Festivities drew the villagers to the market, next to the church, and I was hungry for real food. Not hunted food. Prepared food, by a woman.

"So I found myself in the market. While hawkers tried to sell me on charms or religious articles, she approached me. Her hair was dark and long and her eyebrows sharpened. I have never seen black eyes like hers before. Blacker than the brown of her hair.

'So this is what it took to smoke you out?' she said.

"She knew me, I could tell. My instincts had failed me. She surprised me with her recognition. She surprised me by how much she could see into my thoughts, and I had never met her in person before. I tried to play the role of the ignorant by observing some shelled trinkets sprawled on a board before me. She pursued me.

'I have been waiting for you.'

'You have me mistaken.'

'I know who you are. My father pays you for your work.'

'I don't know your father.'

'Yes, you do. He pays you to create fear.'

"The more she spoke, the more I wanted to escape. I had left one prison to be entrapped in another. I felt myself suffocating the more she stared at me. The more she leaned into me.

'I have been waiting for you here. I will find you in other places when the time comes.'

"She spoke to me as if she knew she would bear my child already. She slid her arms around my waist and placed her head on my chest. I didn't move, I simply stood still. She then left and disappeared into the crowd. She had planted an evil seed in me. And from that point forward, I could think of only her. I searched for her late into the night, after she had disappeared from the festival. When I returned to the camp, everyone dropped to the ground praising Allah.

"Some took a bullet to the head for not watching me close enough, for not protecting me the way they should have. I believed I would never see her again, until she found me in the desert."

The cargo truck stops and the sliding door opens with a loud rattle. The bright light of the new day blinds him temporarily. When his eyes dry some more, The Messenger recognizes the Valley of Kaa behind the men about to inspect the contents of the truck. When the outlines of these men clear, The Messenger identifies the border man, the general, whom he had paid to cross. The official recognizes The Messenger as well and is shocked to see him sitting next to Kashif.

The Messenger realizes there is no need to pay this man this time around. He walks into the truck and approaches Kashif himself.

He says, "I am sorry, I didn't know."

Kashif doesn't respond. He looks over to The Messenger.

"Prepare yourself."

"For what?"

"For the desert where she found me."

Day 32

Crossing the border is easier than driving by it on a secret road. The door is closed again, so The Messenger assumes they are in Syria. It isn't long before the cargo truck stops and there is calm before a storm of bullets and shattered glass echo within the cab. The Messenger cups his ears. Kashif is numb to any reaction but waiting.

The door slides open and black men in military uniform enter the cargo area. Their skin is spotted with perspiration dots and their tongues are healthy pink when they talk.

The Messenger understands their dialect. They are Nigerian.

Kashif gets up and they lower their rifles. When they see him, they nearly forget The Messenger is present as a potential threat. They offer Kashif their hands and kneel before him like he is their god. They guide him softly, as they would an elderly father, from the cargo truck and curse the former group for transporting such a valuable asset this way. The Messenger translates their anger and Kashif understands it.

They have reached an open plain surrounded by towering trees. The area has been cleared to be used as a dirt runway of sorts. There are single engine planes awaiting them.

"A star must fly amidst the sun," one of the leaders says to Kashif. He doesn't return the appreciation with any words or gestures. Kashif points to The Messenger. The group of men nod. They escort Kashif and The Messenger to a plane third in line of the fleet.

The pilot is honoured to have them on board. He nods to Kashif and The Messenger.

They fly in a cross pattern, The Messenger notices. One plane ahead of them, one behind them, one at either side—their plane in the middle.

Kashif stares out of the circular window. He doesn't seem at all impressed by the royal attention he is receiving. If anything, he seems burdened by its particulars, almost annoyed by the honours. The Messenger decides not to bother him with conversation.

In his own mind, The Messenger remembers the first time he met his own wife. It wasn't as suspicious or dangerous as Kashif's first meeting, although it introduced him to the foreign feeling of having something to lose for the first time in his life.

Karen was sitting on one of those comfortable chairs in the lobby of a hotel in Toronto. He was checking out and preparing to return to Switzerland. There was a line up. So he decided to just sit and wait for the line to disappear. He didn't like waiting.

"I hate to wait in line," she said.

"Me too."

"No one ever sits on these chairs. They are decorative. They remind me of my mother's living room at the front of our house. No one was ever allowed to sit in them, just in case important company came over. But no one was ever important enough to sit in the room. My mother just kept it clean, just in case. And when she died, I did the same, for no other reason but force of habit."

The Messenger appreciated the story. It was honest enough to grab his attention and it reminded him of his own home. Every family had its neurotic habits. Hers was no different. Her hair was light ginger and her skin freckled and she crossed her legs so naturally. She seemed at ease in the lounge chair. They watched people walking in and walking out of the hotel lobby, this area of transition. Concierges greeted them the same way as they said good bye to them on the way out.

The line had diminished to nothing. They remained in the comfortable lounge chairs, as if unable to rise.

"Are you leaving?" she asked.

"I have a flight to catch."

"Oh."

"I was thinking of catching it the next time around if you want to go for a walk."

"I would like that yes." She glanced out the curtain glass to the view of the harbour.

He had left his bags without realizing he did so, or worried if anyone should steal them. The morning was warm on his face and the conversation was as natural and endless as the water was to the horizon. One engine planes floated softly onto the island, one after the other, and they simply watched them land gracefully.

She was a teacher.

He was a peacemaker.

Their dreams were not so dissimilar.

By the end of the morning, and after a rather awkward landing by a single engine plane, he had asked to marry her.

DAY 33

"You have gone from pornographic relationships to romantic ones, is that even possible in the same book," questions The Man. He has returned to keep me company as I wait to see Dr. Risi, the psychiatrist. I scheduled the appointment in secret. I don't want anyone close to me to know I feel separate from my body now. With no control, every movement I make is conscious, even the rhythm of my breaths, which I often count like they are ticks on a stopwatch descending to zero. I don't even believe I picked up the phone to call. It was like the phone summoned me here instead, made the appointment time, and even chauffeured me to the medical center.

Everyone around me is noticeably ill. Why does the psychiatrist, who promises absolute confidentiality, make you wait in a public cesspool of wandering, comparative eyes who spite others "not as sick" but better positioned to see the shift physician on duty. The mortared walls in this cavernous waiting area are painted sealant white. The magazines are colourful despite their germ-infested histories, or old news.

My eyes scan the white ceramic tiled area. Old people and their frustrated adult children. A genderless baby burrowing into the chest of its worried mother. A perfectly healthy-looking teenager texting at record speed.

The scent of alcohol hand cleanser sharpens the air between us like a breathable knife.

The only consolation is that I am waiting in this area on a comfortable leather lounge chair. There is, indeed, something special about sitting in one of these chairs while people come and go through the tunneled subway of sick and healthy stops. Sitting still and peaceful and ignored sinks me further into the worn-out cushion, while others go about the routines of their daily lives.

And just as Karen mentioned in the previous chapter, these chairs in public crossfires are very comfortable. Almost too comfortable for such a setting.

"You're obsessed with chairs now, on top of it all," The Man attempts to provoke me once again. He is growing impatient with the story, I can tell, or maybe he feels slighted as my self-volunteered therapist. I believe he is fed up with my life's digressions and how they disrupt the flow of the fictional narrative I am creating. I can't help it. I need time away from the story to sweeten the juice when I return to it, anyway. And unlike him, I'm not one to draw strength from other people's weaknesses.

"There is no well of hope, or strength, just for your information," he condescends.

"You should try to take advantage of someone else one time. Everyone needs to feel above someone else. It's good for the ego and whatever is good for the ego is good for the centric."

His humour has an edge to it as I sit and wait to see the psychiatrist. I wonder if he will advise medication and if so, if I will accept it. I had always considered medication as a last alternative, while fearing a serotonin dependency.

"Happy pills, happy life," is what I say.

The Man's jokes have fangs now. I am glad to see a nurse, dressed more as a temp or assistant, approach me. She crouches down and speaks to me rather closely, with a voice that resembles the artificial ocean on the sleeping sound machine in Alaia's room.

"The doctor is almost ready to see you. Would you like something soothing, like a warm cup of camomile."

Her offer seems to exclude the caffeine elephant in the room.

"No, I am fine."

When she turns to walk away, I notice how her hourglass shape is the perfect temptation for a lonely doctor absorbing the lonely sins of his patients in the role of a sin eater.

Before long, I hear a door opening but see no one holding it open. The nurse behind her desk nods for me to enter. When I pass her, I am pleased her fragrance is fruitier and less clinical than the scent of hand cleanser in the common waiting area.

The room is warm, cosy and carpeted with a very soft under pad. My feet sink into it like footprints in sand.

Dr. Risi removes his glasses and his sports jacket and with a flat, open palm, points to another comfortable looking sofa chair. I notice he is a rather large man with long arms and legs. His feet are enormously wide and heavy sunk.

When he sits down, he reviews the sheet I filled out earlier.

"You believe you are experiencing a nervous breakdown."

He doesn't question me. He simply releases my writing from the page and into the air like he would a captive dove.

I nod.

"Physical symptoms, random pains, sleepless nights, panic attacks, hearing voices?"

"You sold me out," The Man speaks up from the doctor's chair. He is swiveling around in it like a kid on the tilt-a-whirl.

I nod again.

"You are a teacher."

"Tell him," The Man demands.

"And a writer."

"Oh, you've published?"

"Yes."

"Fiction, I assume."

"Yes."

"Describe these voices."

"Friendly at times, intrusive sometimes."

"On your normal train of thought."

"Yes."

He rubs his chin. He is cleanly shaven although his microphone voice, if you had your eyes closed, would indicate the filter of a grizzled beard.

"You are having a nervous breakdown."

He leans in. No punches held.

I didn't expect him to diagnose me with such ease and temperament. I assumed he had more questions, more personal research to extract from the pocketed area behind my defence mechanisms. He doesn't seem interested in me, though, which surprises and relieves me at the same time.

There is an awkward pause. Does he expect me to say something? I nod again as if condoning an elaboration. He doesn't expand. He retracts into his own thoughts, into the silence. He simply stares at me. His elbows are on his knees now and he is hunched into the huddle of our awkward conversation.

"What is next?" I finally speak up.

"There is nothing next. Only how you regard this space you have carved out for yourself."

"It is hurting me."

"How?"

"I am always afraid. Of little things, like driving at night or out of town on my own. To bigger ones, like cancer scares and dying without notice."

His face absorbs my words and his cheeks appear as if they are chewing upon them. Even the Man is quiet during the conversation. Observant.

"I know you are afraid, just as I know I am afraid. Fear is a tragic conspirator. I'm not going to insult your intelligence and say to get over it. To be thankful for what you have. To focus on the positive. Those solutions are temporary diversions. Your cousin died. He left a family, I presume. He died and his death stole something from you. Your son's Down syndrome stole something from you. Your failures have stolen something from you. Are you aware what has been stolen from you?"

"No. I don't."

"Your ability to forgive yourself."

"What do you mean?"

"Your first marriage ended. You feel guilty about it, no?"

"Yes."

"You are Catholic"—he reviews his notes to be certain—"and I presume you confessed your sins in this regard?"

"Yes."

"You believe God forgives you, no?"

"Yes."

"But you can't forgive yourself."

"Why not?"

His eyebrows lift to the center of his forehead. He knows I have the answer to this question, and so does he, but it is my duty to reveal which battleship has been hit first.

"Because I want to be good."

He reclines into the chair with a deep breath.

"Your desire to be good above your ability to forgive yourself for the bad is deluding you into thinking you are failing your destiny."

"Failing my destiny?"

"Yes. Deep down you want to be greater than you are, and so you don't value what makes you greater than what you are?"

"My weaknesses."

"Precisely. They make you honest, empathetic, sincere, merciful, even heroic. Most of all, they allow you to hear voices. Those voices are speaking to you. They are asking to be heard from the dungeons you have buried them in for the sake of keeping your clean walls upright. Forgive yourself. You are human and your humanity is begging for you to listen above the lies of your dreams."

"This guy is pretty good. Didn't expect him to be my murderer," The Man says under his breath.

As Dr. Risi whispers to his nurse, The Man is anxious to distract me from the session.

"Quit your job, Dean. That's the first step, trust me. The kids aren't getting easier to entertain with all of their distractions. No man should work in the same place for thirty years. It kills his spirit."

I don't answer him. The Man's voice is panic stricken, desperate, unlike the doctor's.

"Let's talk about your story while we wait," advises The Man. "Okay, terrorist groups are taking their turns kidnapping Kashif and The Messenger and it appears as if they are heading to Nigeria, of all places. I'm assuming you are basing this on your research of the top five terrorist groups on the planet."

I really don't feel like talking to The Man right now.

"When will I re-enter the story?"

"I don't know yet. I may have a spot for you in a future scene."

"You sound like a director at an audition now, letting me down easy."

"Listen. There are parts of this story evolving on their own. I am creating it, but sometimes you hit a system and you have to rely on your instincts more than your preparation."

"Who are you kidding? You are an irresponsible creator."

He is upset and I do feel sorry for him. He has watched the story unfold and I believe he has become envious of my protagonist, who is earning his station.

The Man has moved across the room, by the windows now.

"This isn't much of a view," he says as he stares out onto a country road and parking lot. I can tell from the tone of his voice he is trying to discredit this new expert in my life.

"Did you ever see yourself here, fifteen years ago, right after you graduated with your M.A. in English and Creative Writing. It's a shame to have that degree on your wall, in your office. I look at it a lot and think what a shame it is."

The Man has resorted once again to insults. He is the personification of my inability to forgive myself. He is The Man responsible for populating my fears from within.

Although, to some degree, I couldn't agree with The Man more where it concerns my education. After I graduated with my degree, I thought I would live and breathe as a writer and as a writer only. Those lofty dreams floated away so fast after our last poetry reading at The Eclectic. I remember making the audience take notice that night. I felt ready to take on the world with stories only to realize that stories bear little fruit on the tree of life, although they do feed you lies about yourself.

"I'll try my best to get you back in," I promise The Man.

"If you have to force me in, don't do it. It isn't worth it. This may be the last story you ever write and I don't want you to ruin it for me."

"Dean?"

"Yes."

"Do you have anything more to say?"

Dr. Risi is sitting in front of me again. His voice is soft and dismissive.

I feel like everyone is staring at me except there is only one other real person in the room with me.

"How do I do it?"

"Forgive yourself?"

"Yes."

"By accepting, deep down, that you are only you. No more, no less."

When I leave his office, all of the cars in the parking lot have disappeared. My mouth is dry. My muscles softened as if from a massage, or bruising. The Man has disappeared as well and I wonder if he has run away for good. He was always around when I felt most weak and I worry if this little visit to the doctor lessened his powers, like incidental kryptonite.

On the drive home, I want to call my wife. I call and the phone rings to voicemail. She never picks up on the first call.

Day 34

"We are going to a place of many stories," Kashif explains on the plane. The engine is loud and the pilots are silent and armed.

"How do you know where we are going?"

"Don't you? These men are Nigerian. They form one of the most powerful terror groups on the planet. Can't you tell from the organization?"

The Messenger feels like an idle student in this global classroom. He is familiar with Nigeria, in particular, its older language, which was seldom used at the U.N. He is also aware that English is the dominant language in Nigeria, used in schools and at the government level. The Messenger remembers the national motto of Nigeria, "Peace and Unity, Strength and Progress."

"There are deep jihadist roots in Nigeria," Kashif exhales. His voice is not louder than the engines. It finds a communication silence in between the roar and rhythm of the propellers.

"You will see no more death at this level. Only negotiation," assures Kashif.

Although The Messenger believes every word Kashif imparts to him, he spites him for holding secrets. Kashif doesn't reveal until he feels the need to and The Messenger is at a loss, made to feel condescended to in this relationship. In an attempt to impress him as an adult, The Messenger recalls his education out loud.

"Are you alluding to the Hausa states and the conversion of the Kanem–Bornu Empire to Islam in the eleventh century?"

Kashif is stunned for a second.

"You are insulted."

"I am not a child. I don't need to be led."

"Believe me, I am not doing so to maintain power over you."

"You could have fooled me."

"Information is best when it is timely, don't you agree?"

"No, I don't. Information is best when you know it enough to use it."

"But we don't know everything all at once. There needs to be a balance between our ignorance and knowledge for us to maintain curiosity, to stay sharp in the eyes of adversity."

He does his best not to show an agreeable face but The Messenger can't help but agree with Kashif. His manner is persuasive. His words are also transformative, like his appearance. He is a fluid man who is constantly sculpting or moulding himself into another shape.

"When you are colonized as many times as these people, you develop an appetite to fight. This is a dangerous, tribal group. They kill children in schools and innocent women without blinking an eye. Their statements are extreme. Their soil is softened by blood and war. They don't eat with the left hand."

Once again, Kashif mentions the metaphor of eating in the context of killing and war. This appetite he alludes to confuses The Messenger and it reminds him of the horrific story of Kashif's recruitment as a young boy. This link to eating is something The Messenger can't seem to get his head around. Why is it significant that they don't eat with the left hand?

The plane begins its descent and The Messenger can see that they are flying over an urban center. It appears as if they will land atop a building.

"It is the ritual of signifying a celebration."

"What are they celebrating?"

"More money."

Kashif is ashamed when he says this. He looks away from The Messenger to stare out the window. Civilians are waving at the planes flying low over the city centre. The Messenger finally understands what is happening now. Kashif is now the commodity, in the same way oil and petroleum is to Nigeria. Kashif is a tradable asset, which means this is not the last stop on their journey. This is the trading post, a place of acquisition and transaction. Kashif will be auctioned off to the highest bidder for a monetary amount and that highest bidder will have the child they are looking for.

When the plane lands, The Messenger can hear music and the stomping of feet. The plane shakes, guns are fired into the sky, and there is Peace and Unity outside, Strength and Progress. Kashif takes a breath and transforms his face into a public persona, similar to a political figure visiting a place in his constituency for the first time to attain votes.

The door of the plane opens and loud air enters the cabin like an announcement. The Messenger watches Kashif being led to the light at the door. When he is revealed within its frame, the noise increases to a point of nearly tipping the plane onto its side. The ground rumbles and The Messenger rises to stay close to him.

DAY 35

The Man of Many Wives has a baby face, smooth and silky, young and ageless, shiny and dark. He has four wives and they rotate around him like black angels in white sheets. Their eyes are yellow and they respect the space around their husband. This is the leader of the group. He approaches Kashif before the apparent forlorn prophet reaches the last step from the plane. He kneels, wipes away the sandy dirt with his right hand and kisses the ground before Kashif steps on it. The militant audience erupts with applause. The Man of Many Wives rises and kisses Kashif's hand gently. His wives pull flower petals from underneath their garments to form a fragrant path for him. The Messenger feels uncomfortable, unnoticed in this ceremony, until Kashif stops. He waves him on and when The Messenger places his feet in his footsteps, Kashif offers him his hand. He holds his hand as a brother or lover would, as they follow The Man of Many Wives and his predestined path of flowers.

The trail leads them to a city square, surrounded by buildings, cobblestoned around a grand fountain. There is a platform set up before the fountain.

The Man of Many Wives walks up the platform to introduce Kashif. He describes him very eloquently as a man who has seen God, as a man who will ascend one day as a true prophet of their generation. Kashif is unmoved by these words of praise and acclamation. They don't penetrate him. If anything, he is bored by the ceremony, by the appreciation. It means nothing to him.

It is nighttime when The Man of Many Wives escorts them to a room in the compound. It is highly decorated with items speaking the language of excess and wealth. Gold faucets, golden chandeliers, gold speckled marble tiles.

His face, like Kashif's, has changed by night. He is no longer the public leader, the humble demonstrator, or even The Man of

Many Wives. He has come alone. He invites Kashif and The Messenger to sit at the gold-laced wooden table. His voice has also changed. It is unfeeling now, almost mathematical.

"We are taking bids and then the negotiation will begin."

"Thank you for your hospitality."

"I am pleased you are ours for the moment. You have vaulted our value."

Kashif doesn't say anything. It is obvious. The Man of Many Wives is about to leave the room when Kashif stops him.

"You have many children, true?"

"Yes, four wives and fourteen children."

"You are a lucky man."

"Yes, I am blessed. Please refrain from insulting me further."

"They will eat you one day," Kashif predicts.

The Man of Many Wives leaves the room, obviously upset. It is the first time The Messenger sees Kashif as aggressive on this peculiar journey. He doesn't understand the insult at all. To The Messenger, Kashif's questions were small talk, polite and cordial. But The Man of Many Wives received them differently.

Before asking him, The Messenger thinks about it some more. Why would The Man of Many Wives be insulted about a family question?

"Because he knows I saw through him from the beginning. He is proud to have captured to me, but I told him I surrendered to him. He is using me to further his group, I am using him to further my search. He is a liar by trade, and so am I, but my truth makes me more real to our destinies. He is aware now that I am aware of his story."

Although a language specialist and a premier translator, The Messenger feels inferior to this code language amongst them. They speak terror and fear, and their mode of communication is not to clarify, but to riddle and hide. They become their art, and their art aims to stay on the wall of civilization longer than any other.

Kashif points to the bags delivered to the room.

"Take a shower and clean up. It won't be long now. We will be sold and bought and then delivered to the council."

Kashif enters the bathroom and closes the door.

DAY 36

My first son, from my first marriage, is down for the weekend. We are celebrating his belated birthday due to the fact it didn't fall on one of my visiting weekends. It is nice to see he is back on track at school. We talk on the return drive from London and he fills me in on the meeting he and his mother had with his teacher at school.

Apparently, he needs to stay clear of a very popular friend who is distracting him from his studies. In the same key, he is very creative, according to his teacher, with the potential to be the top student in class. I nearly laugh at the subjective way he sees himself.

"Daddy, I'm going to be better," he assures me. "I'm going to start working out more and getting in shape too. I can't waste my talents, Daddy," he says seriously, and I am happy he feels better about himself.

My wife and I have made up since our last argument. She broke down in tears and apologized for the cruel words she said the night she compared my chosen career path with the more successful options my brothers pursued.

I understand that attending each and every therapy session for Tobias has taken its toll on her. When I fell in love with her, I loved her most for her enthusiasm about family and the adventures we would have growing a big one by today's urban standards. Neither of us anticipated the challenges lurking in these familial dreams. Nor did we foresee how those challenges would interfere with our own relationship, which we both thought invincible.

Unfortunately, she lost the innocent belief that everything is going to be all right. I try every day to remind her we have everything to be grateful for and many days she is the one convincing me, but it isn't healthy on either end, I suppose. The assurance begins to sound like lies when compared to the reality of our situation. One son estranged three hours away, another challenged by his inability to walk, eat and go potty, even at the age of five, with the other two innocent of what responsibilities lie before them in the future. When we make up, we both agree that we need to be more positive and to value the little things— our daily and adventurous bath routines, the cartoonish characters of our children, the way they love us in return. We are very blessed and the air is clear before my son's belated birthday party.

That same air becomes foggy again when we celebrate it at my parents' home. It is always loud when we celebrate events at my parents' house. All of the grandchildren are virtually in the same room and the noise levels are unbearable. Within the chaos of trying to get them fed, refereed after innocuous conflicts, and arranging them together at the table to sing happy birthday, I overhear a conversation my son Aidan has with my father, and once more I am saddened.

My father comments to my son that he is getting older.

"Pretty soon you are going to drive to see us," he remarks.

"That's four years away, Nonno," my son giggles it off. He is happy to have everyone's attention at the party, even though he said we didn't have to celebrate it on the drive back from London. I told him he wasn't old enough yet to complain about celebrating his birthday and he didn't resist any further.

In the same conversation, my father asks my son what he wants to be in his life. They assume I am not listening or over-hearing the conversation because I am trying to get my one-year-old daughter to sit on my lap and drink from my glass cup.

"I want to write stories," my son says.

This admission stabs me so deep I feel physical pain in my back.

"Maybe you should be a doctor, or a lawyer," my father responds in a broken, accented whisper.

"They make good money, they have their own office, peo-ple respect them," my father says even lower, pulling my son closer to show affection at the same time.

"But I like writing stories. I read a lot of books, Nonno."

I pretend to ignore them and their conversation, even though I can sense both are looking at me. I am not even insulted by my father's words. I have known these feelings since my mother first told my father I wanted to write stories. My father is a rag to riches success story. He immigrated to Canada when he was sixteen. He worked shitty, automotive, mechanic jobs, only to realize the potential wealth in car recycling. He purchased a building when I was merely one, mortgaging everything he owned, including our house, at 18% (I have heard the story many times), and risked everything only to see it off with great dividends. As a result of his struggles, he forced us to stay in school. He wanted us to have "clean" jobs; he insisted, and he envied the lawyer's offices he often visited to broker deals, their suited attires, the bills they presented him with, and of course the exorbitant amounts bolded on those invoices.

My father never understood my passion for writing. He could never relate to it since he was virtually illiterate in this country. My mother, who immigrated at seven years old, went to school in Canada and together they formed a can't-miss partnership. My mother handled accounts, my father took risks. My father never respected teachers, and yet I became one. He never understood the economic benefits of writing, because he never read a book. All he ever preached was developing a good name, for business sake, and both of my brothers followed suit, which made their pursuits more relatable to him. I never spite my father for never asking about my writing career. I know he is proud of the man I have become, but I also know he wishes I could have become someone more important in a suit.

Although I am happy my son defends his interests to my father, I see my mistakes repeated in another time zone. I've taken some portal time machine only to see my first dreams in an objective light and they appear saturated in delusion.

After this secret conversation, my son finds his way to me. He knows I am busy with his one-year-old sister but he gives me a back hug. My father watches to see how affectionate he is with me and I can read envy in his eyes now, or disappointment. I'm not sure. I know my father doesn't think his first son successful on an economic level. And now, his first grandson is following the rabbit down the same, darkened hole.

I anticipate another anxiety-ridden night, but I don't feel sorry for myself anymore or the decisions I have made. I find out a week later that my son also had a conversation with my mother that night, one I didn't overhear.

"He thinks you work too hard. He told me. He's a bright boy. Even though he isn't here all of the time."

"I know. I need to spend more time with him when he is down. Some more one on one time."

"You know what else he told me?"

"What, Mom?"

"He said, 'My Daddy does all of these different jobs to make money for us, but he loves writing the most. I can tell, that's what he wants to do more than anything. He is happy when he is writing.'"

My mother's face is tragic when she relates this to me. It wrinkles with a lifetime of concern. Aside from my first novel being published, both of my parents don't look kindly on awards, or award nominations that garner very little economic return. They have never understood why I spend so much time doing something that doesn't make me money, or improve the future of my kids. I expect more criticism from my mother. As the first born, I have always received it in bushels. This time around she is impressed by something.

"He really admires and loves you," she says, almost breaking into tears.

I know where I get my sadness from and I worry I will be having the same conversation with my son, many years away, when he reveals his greatest passion and dreams aren't really working out for him as he first expected.

"I'm sorry things haven't worked out, Mom."

I am alluding to so many of my mistakes when I say this to my mother. My failed career choices, my failed first marriage, my inability to fulfill the dream I promised I would prove them wrong with. I am old enough not to blame them for their lack of faith in my abilities. And I am wise enough to realize your choices are yours and yours only. They have nothing to do with anyone else. They are a part of your destiny. And yet I continue to believe that even this book I am writing will save everything. Like one book can alter the course of time. Like a word placed in the right spot can shift the axis of the earth. And who knows, maybe it already has since I've written it down.

The Man doesn't show up to my son's birthday party. I didn't invite him and perhaps he knows I need to spend some time away from our conversations. Also, I don't need to be reminded not to feel sorry for myself. No one likes a pity party but the person who craves pity in the first place. And like most cravings, they can surely turn into addictions, or worse yet, chronic syndromes.

My son is very grateful for the gifts he receives on his birthday. They are thoughtful gifts and I don't have to prompt him to say thank you for them. He feels appreciated by the family he may often believe forgets about him when he isn't around. He feels grateful to have a father he admires. I don't want him to be a writer and I wish he could be so innocent of faulty dreams forever.

DAY 37

"So, are you going to finish this story or what?"

The Man wakes me in the middle of the night. It is four AM and he can't even wait seventeen minutes more, when he knows I habitually jolt to have my panic attacks. He is impatient, almost edgy. He is in a hurry to be, before he disappears from my memory. Or maybe he is anxious to enter the story, although I haven't figured out a way yet to get him back into it.

"You can't get so distracted now. You have to finish up strong. The Messenger and Kashif are about to be sold to another terrorist group and they will present themselves before the council. By the way, this mysterious council confuses me. I don't see it in your research notes."

"So you admit to reading my research notes?"

"Of course. It makes me feel like I'm reading those 'pick your ending' books. Remember, you used to like them as a kid?"

"How do you know that?"

"Is this argument necessary again? What does it matter what I know, as long as you know I know it. We are family, no?"

I never thought of him this way. My creation as family, and yet this domestic metaphor is prevalent in every association with God as a creator. His creations are children, he is a father, or possibly a mother, one and the same.

"The Council is something I read into when I sifted through the Al-Qaeda research," I admit. No family secrets here.

"The ones found in Iraq, after the liberation?"

"Yes."

"Where?"

Although I can't see The Man, I can imagine him shuffling through my papers, although in real time I know they remain still in various piles in my office.

"The torture explanations are written in presentation format, as if prepared for a specific audience, a selective audience. Each torture depicted in those drawings and the accompanying text is intended to impress someone else. Like it was an experiment or something. And there were discoveries made of an ethereal nature. In those side notes, I caught a misprint, something scratched out. After staring at it and blowing it up, I found an insignia. A council insignia."

"So it was documentation intended to impress a specific group?" The Man is thinking aloud.

"Yes. Although I didn't write it down anywhere, I found the same insignia elsewhere, in some other writings. And then I discovered the designation of the council in some irrelevant research on The Illuminati."

"Oh my, is this what your book is coming to, another version of The Da Vinci Code."

"Very funny. This Council exists in absolute secrecy, above levels of government and laws, as an oligarchy of sorts."

"Much better, more like Orwell now," The Man comments.

"No, not like Orwell. This Council is not consumed with control or power. Just immortality."

The Man is silent and I believe I have earned my seventeen minutes of additional sleep. This new information doesn't satisfy him. He is relentless, almost desperate.

"You still have to introduce the kid, that's if you want to make him real, so you have a lot of work to do. You know it is always hard to finish a novel and you have passed your deadline for the first draft. Next semester is about to start. You will have new classes and the worries of the literacy test. Not to mention your big grievance decision. Do you want to do this or not?"

The Man sounds like a motivational coach. He never sounded so desperate and impassioned about the finish line.

"What do you mean, making the child real? Of course the child is real."

"I don't see any research about a miracle child anywhere. Is he solely a concoction, a wildcard element to the story?"

"You don't believe this child exists? He is the reason for the journey. He is the ultimate justification of cause for the council. This child exists in the same way Sister Carmelina existed."

"Sister Carmelina? Who are you talking about now?"

The Man is confused and I feel empowered that he didn't know the inspiration for this character. He doesn't know everything happening in my mind and my imagination. My newfound pride reveals it to him.

"Sister Carmelina cured my brother."

"Of what?"

"Of a swollen gland. When my brother was a child, his one salivary gland jutted out like a goiter. My mother thought it was a tumor. The specialists at Sick Kids Hospital couldn't explain it. At one point, he could barely swallow. It was nearly suffocating him. So my religious mother decided to take us all to a hospital in Tripoli. There was a nun bedridden there. She had been bedridden her entire life, since she was a little girl. I remember the visit. Her skin was so white and her hair so dark. We entered her hospital room as a family and she was already speaking to my mother about my brother's condition. She then raised her hand and placed it on the swollen gland. My family watched as she fell into a deep, trancelike sleep. I was younger, but I remember trying to see if she flinched, or moved, or squinted. Not even her eyelashes twitched. She was frozen while her hand was glued to my brother's gland. It lasted quite some time. And then she woke up softly.

"The next morning, my brother woke us all screaming from the bathroom. He felt a little rock under his tongue. It was attached to the bottom of his tongue and plain to the sight. My mother took him to the hospital and with a simple cut, the doctor removed it.

"The doctor couldn't explain the phenomenon. The specialists at Sick Kids were using words like miraculous.

"The church is trying to canonize her now and she has many miracles to her name."

The Man is quiet after I recount this memory. Even though I can't see him, I can tell he is rolling his eyes.

"This is the inspiration for the kidnapped child?" The Man is not converted by my personal story.

"Yes. I have learned that the least suspected are the most expected."

"And if Kashif finds this child, his daughter will be healed? What about him? Will he be healed of all of his past transgressions?"

"I haven't thought about it yet," I admit honestly.

"Well, shouldn't you? You are the author of this story. This is your main character. Is it possible to remove your past sins with one, swift, sleight of hand? Reminds me of those born-agains. Yeah, sure, it's easy to say you have given up your vices after you've lived an entire lifetime enjoying them. How convenient it is to be born again, just before you die and are destined for Hell."

"I haven't decided Kashif's end, just like I haven't decided how the story will end. If I did so, I would be leading the story to the end instead of creating it honestly."

"Does a writer care more about his integrity than his reader? You are both, no? Writer and Reader? As a reader, how long have you idealized stories, believed they were written just for you, for no profit or gain but to make you dream of writing your own someday?"

"What is your point?"

"You are doing the same as a writer now! This book is too honest and will be silenced. Lies are easier sold than truths. History has proven this time and time again. You don't want to get dirty, that's your problem. To win is to cheat, to cheat is to outsmart, to outsmart is to be ahead, to be ahead is to reach the end before anyone else. Moral victories are just that, moral—weak—soft—invisible and, eventually, silent."

"Art has always been an appreciation of silence," I defend.

"Tell that to the person who is making money from your art, enough to allow him to make more of it. While you rot in a day job hoping someone will discover how brilliant you are and save you from your excuses. Heck, you started off this novel saying you weren't going to write what an audience expected. You should do as you promised. Burn this fucking story, right after you rob it."

My daughter enters the room and her high pitched voice makes me flinch. I fear she might have heard a profanity before her time but then remember that only I seem to hear The Man. Unless she has some child-like sixth sense.

"Hi Daddy. Hi Daddy. Hi Daddy. Hi Daddy."

She sounds like a skipping record, except she likes the sound of her own voice.

"Hi, Alaia. How is my sweetie doing?"

I pick her up and place her on my lap. I love when she leans back onto my chest. I can smell her hair and marvel at the tiny touch of her finger tips resting in the palm of my hand.

"Don't write the ending for her to read one day. Write it even though it may hurt her one day to think her Daddy might have sinned beyond her dream of you."

She squirms her way off of my lap as if hearing her mother calling her elsewhere. She stops and stares at me before she leaves. Did she hear what The Man said? Or does she see her father in the preliminary stages of schizophrenia.

"Bye Daddy."

Day 38

I stall on the scene before my blurry ending. I can feel, by instinct, where the story is going, what end it will reach but I am stumped on this transition scene. This scene will be the catalyst scene, the one propelling the story with speed to its finale.

It takes me a few days to mull it over. In that span, I spend some time with my children. I return to my routine of bathing them at night. Reading stories with them before bedtime. Shuttling them around to swimming lessons and soccer camps and ice skating. The scene doesn't come to me right away. This is the first time I have hit a wall as the writer of the story and The Man is nowhere to be found. He doesn't offer any advice or help. He seldom does when I really need it. I suppose I created him this way. To capitalize upon a weakness but not to contribute to a strength.

I left the story with Kashif reminding The Messenger they were close to their meeting with the council. The Man of Many Wives doesn't impress Kashif. Why should he? He is a carbon copy, a cheaper version of himself who takes pride in the fact he has something in common with the legend he kidnaps. Kashif recognizes this pride from a mile away. He doesn't appreciate it, nor does he consider himself greater than The Man of Many Wives. This journey is a chore into the past for Kashif. He has grown to prefer his visits to the hospital, the routine of seeing his daughter, although he will never admit this flaw in the presence of The Messenger or anyone else. He is also aware that this softness is recognizable to those with instincts as refined as his. If he finds himself in front of the council, they will smell him out and devour him. For this entire journey he has been keeping this secret away from The Messenger. This new fascination with his own weaknesses.

Kashif had lived an entire life made cold by warm blood on his hands, knowing full well, that with every murder he committed, he was becoming more and more numb to his own humanity. Similar to Macbeth, he had reached a stage where he couldn't even react to a "night shriek." "Blood will have blood," he used to repeat to himself. Now, that same man is only a costume, only a shell he is trying with increased effort to sell to everyone he encounters along the way.

The idea of this miracle child fascinates him as well. The personification of strength from weakness. The boy doesn't walk. He is disabled, Kashif believes. And yet, he performs miracles. How is that so? Never, in his previous life, would he believe in such a deliberate contradiction in nature. The bad should cancel out the good, or vice versa.

Kashif fears he has been inadvertently influenced by the Maronites he has hidden amongst for so many years. Their Saviour on a cross, naked, bleeding, thought to be a criminal. How could the same man be a God of power and strength, able to defeat death and recreate life in another dimension? This contradiction, similar to the child's, is so obvious but so true in its conception.

He never saw strength this way before, this softly, the flesh in it. For years, he had only seen the bones of it, the calcium deposits making fractures stronger after being broken.

In the bathroom, alone, he is expecting someone to break and enter.

(This is what comes to me in the shower. I woke up feeling my entire body tired and weak, almost brittle. Perhaps I am getting sick again, or maybe I am making myself sick. Either way, I am sweating naked in the mirror when I place Kashif in a similar scene.)

Kashif knows The Messenger is expecting him, fully dressed in his suit, outside the bathroom. Kashif is in the bathroom alone. He dims the lights. He is naked in front of the mirror. Scars line his skin in random patterns. Some seem to resemble letters, even words, or a canvas of scratched in margin notes better suited for his own story. He can't help himself from seeing such scars differently now. They are no longer battle scars. Symbolic of strength. No, no, no. He feels the one by his rib cage, formed from a twisted knife. It is silky smooth and soft, but strong enough to hold things together.

His instincts dictate one thing, his heart another. He knows to expect someone to break into the bathroom any minute. Not from the door, but from the window. The sounds of festivities are below. There is celebration in the streets. There is hilarity in the forested areas surrounding the village. And there is condensation on the windows. Someone will appear soon. His instincts are rarely incorrect. Someone will enter, uninvited, to take his blood.

This is the reason why he dug up the box of needles from his cave closet. He didn't know it then, but his instincts prompted the retrieval. His box of needles and glass bottles. Blood samples to prove he is the same man who defeated enemy armies with the stroke of an ingenious idea. Blood samples with his DNA, the only way to prove his identity. The identity he had expertly kept secret for so long. The identity not even agencies trained to investigate could determine. The identity of a chameleon, whose skin changes and whose blood stays the same.

There is a knock at the door.

"Are you all right?" It is the Messenger. He is worried in his voice and expecting the next stage of the journey.

"I am fine."

As he says this in the mirror, Kashif observes how his face moves, how it changes and contorts with every word. This is how others must see him, he determines. This is what makes them afraid.

In the corner of the mirror, a black figure emerges from the window. As silent as Kashif's skin in the mirror, he is wearing a mask. His body is athletic in black and he moves slanted, like a shadow against a wall. He is not a threat. He is only a technician. Kashif doesn't flinch to be found naked, exposed, and vulnerable. After considering the man on the cross, the god on the cross, he is learning a newfound strength in this apparent weakness of exposure.

The man in the black costume finds the black box with the needles and capsules. How does he know his tools await him on site? Kashif wonders. How is this man aware of the instincts that prompted Kashif to bring the box along in the first place?

"Lie down."

There is a towel on the bathroom floor. It is dampened from the shower. Kashif lies on it as he would an operating table.

The technician in the black costume expertly removes the needles. He attaches the glass capsules and injects one of the needles into the softest landscape of green veins, on the flipside of Kashif's elbow.

He lines up the bottles on the sink. Kashif counts them. One, two, three. Why do they require so much blood from him to determine if he is the real thing, the man they built an industry upon? Is there another purpose for the blood?

"Blood will have blood," he thinks again. Are they trying to match the quantity shed on his behalf?

The Messenger opens the door and he is fearful of the scene or just fearful of the man in black extracting blood out of Kashif's arm. Or maybe he is fearful of a naked man lying supine on the bathroom floor, too helpless to move with the needle in his arm.

He doesn't say anything. He doesn't react. He doesn't understand, but he is all right with it if Kashif is voluntary. He has learned a lot from this journey, Kashif believes. To be aware of the details surrounding a story. To see them as reflections of character rather than setting and props.

The Messenger politely leaves the room to secure the ritual privacy.

The number of bottles on the sink is ten and counting.

DAY 39

"I am no master writer or critic, by any means, but you changed the point of view near the end of the story? That's a no, no. You're not established enough to assume the license to do this. That last scene was entirely written from Kashif's perspective. A definite faux pas."

"Did you just say 'faux pas'?"

I tease The Man because, as I first noted in my preface, I don't care to please. In order to move a story, sometimes you have to take a risk. I wanted that scene to be emotionally detonating. Kashif submitting blood on the bathroom floor like a person. Counting capsules of his own blood on the counter.

In my mind's eye, he was never the beast of his reputation. In my mind's eye, I realize he is a sinner, as evil as one may be, but he is still human. And humanity is always the salvation point.

"You're not going to pull it off, Dean. You can't make him a hero because you feel sorry for him, or because you have fallen in love with the character. Justice is much bigger than your imagination. The balance of good and evil existed long before your conception of it. He doesn't deserve to survive this excursion. The Messenger, on the other hand, is redeemable."

I don't appreciate The Man offering his two cents, although at this point his is a much steeper investment. He is right, in some respect. I want to dimensionalize this character some more before the ending. So far, I have developed him as an instinctive warrior who sees terror as a form of art to be valued in its intricate design. I think I've also established him as a father, just like me and many others, who is concerned first and foremost with the health of his child. This aspect, I believe, makes him relatable, but also pathetic enough to change. Up until this point, he has manipulated himself physically. He has undergone surgeries and breached extremes to adopt a chameleon role for various, survival reasons. Only now is he changing from within. This metamorphosis is his redemption, I believe. This changing of the guard from the inside out.

"I don't believe it," The Man interposes. He is downright harassing me now as my class is writing their exams. They are quiet. Every once in a while, though, one or two of my students regard me strangely like they are eavesdropping on the conversation.

"If I were a reader, I would find it very hard to believe Kashif is capable of such humanity."

"But aren't the greatest sinners most capable?"

I almost say this out loud or rather under my breath. Because it is so quiet in the classroom, some of my students hear it. Or maybe they are looking up from the exam because they are stressed to the point of distraction.

"What is it, Emily?" I ask out loud.

"Nothing, just thought I saw another grey hair."

I get up from my desk and pace between rows pretending I am proctoring the exam properly. My students are working hard and I am thinking hard.

I nearly skip to my desk to resume my scene. I'm going to stay in Kashif's perspective if only to annoy The Man further.

Kashif wakes up after The Messenger places a cold cloth on his face.

"You passed out. Must have been the bloodletting."

Kashif realizes The Messenger is upset with him. His sarcasm indicates a lack of trust in the grander picture.

"I don't want to explain. Not yet."

"Who was that? He nearly drained you of blood. Look?"

The Messenger, when helping Kashif to the sitting position, pulls loose skin away from his forearm bone.

"I don't know why they needed so much. It is something beyond my identity or purpose."

"Do you need help getting dressed?" The Messenger asks.

"No, just help me get onto my feet."

Kashif feels like he has entered another body unlike his own. It doesn't respond well to stimulus. The limbs, although bloodless, are heavy in movement.

He returns to the sink, washes his face and notices his skin has paled in tone, dramatically. The bloodletting transformed him into the unexpected likeness of his natural self. It seemed to reverse the many surgeries. He sees the man he used to be in the mirror now. The one with an appetite for destruction. The one intent on destroying meaning and routine and norms and anything worthy of peace.

"Someone came to the door. He said the pilot has arrived?"

Kashif realizes the negotiation has finalized. He leaves the bathroom and finds the suit he stitched on the table. He dresses as quickly as he can and returns to the mirror to ensure he appears strong and not weakened by the absence of his own blood.

"I didn't see him leave. The man in black. I didn't hear him come or go?"

"He isn't the pilot. He is another man. The negotiation has ended."

When they leave the room it is early morning. The festivities are dead and the world is asleep. Kashif walks ahead of The Messenger. He gains strength with every step down a corridor. Although he is weakened, he believes his instincts have strengthened as a result of his body's attempt at recovering itself.

He knows the pilot is employed by the most powerful terror organization, the one directly linked to and on the right hand of the governing council.

The pilot is dressed in naval military uniform. He is young and angular.

Kashif understands that the final terrorist group is waiting on the plane for him. The Messenger stands close by. He appears to be looking for The Man of Many Wives but that man has already been taken care of. He has no reason to be polite anymore. No one dies at this level. These are merely transactions, investments with returns. Numbers trounce pleasantries at this level and Kashif doesn't feel the need to educate The Messenger. He believes The Messenger will figure this out for himself.

"Let me lead you to the plane."

The pilot marches down the stairwell and to a shiny limousine. The chauffeur is waiting by the door. The Messenger, Kashif and the pilot are escorted to a private plane gleaming on its own runway.

Another accordion stairway leads to an open door up above.

Kashif and The Messenger follow the pilot up the steps. When they enter the plane another group is expecting them.

"To the ruins," a young man speaks up in the direction of the pilot.

The pilot nods and Kashif moves to the seat prepared for him.

Day 40

"You have the child," are Kashif's first words as he takes a seat in the plane. There are three young men sitting in the cabin with him. The Messenger is seated across from him, curious. The three young men don't resemble each other. They are not brothers, or part of a brotherhood, like the other groups. These men are educated from various corners of the world. The screens of laptop computers flicker against the screens of their lighter faces. The man who speaks first is fair-skinned, almost freckled by the eyes. His accent is educated, private school British. He doesn't act like he is caught in a lie. He is transparent, through and through.

"Not with us on this plane, but yes, we have the child. And yes, he does perform miracles at our command."

Kashif nods. He knows the man who speaks for the other two is the most powerful terrorist on the planet now. A position he once held. He is the future. He is dressed in a business suit as well. There is an aura about him not requiring a formal introduction of names. His presence introduces and speaks on his behalf. He is special. He is not weakened by anything, most especially a conscience. His demeanour is razor sharp as are the creases of his suit and his jawline. The other two type feverishly on their computers. Their business is not his business.

"I will not thank you or praise you like the others, if you don't mind."

"I wouldn't expect any different," answers Kashif.

"I understand who you are, why you are valuable to the council, but your history is of no value to me. I create my own set apart from what you have created."

Kashif is well aware of the man's confidence, which may appear unappreciative, ungrateful or downright arrogant to The

Messenger. He also deduces the angles this man is presenting him. He is invincible, just as he was one day in the past. He believes himself immortal, which gives him hierarchy over all human beings. He has convinced himself he is greater than his own imagination of himself.

Heavy silences seem to press the plane down to a lower elevation. Kashif doesn't feel the need to talk. Neither does this leader. The others are working on their computers. In the reflection of the plane windows, and in this cocoon of tan leather upholstery, Kashif can see, hear and smell them creating stories via media. These are storytellers furthering the legend of power. Kashif knows what terrorist group this is. The young man was right. It is a group distinct from the concepts of terror he first created. This group prides itself on promotion, publicity, video—visual statements. This group creates fear with story, with film, with shock value. They stage executions as in days of old and then use such episodes to disseminate fear into online veins. Kashif considers his ways old in their new context. Yet, they are artists, just the same. They simply understand the theory of distribution.

The plane descends upon a city of ruins, an area of stone rubble, collapsed buildings and perpetual dust rising to cloud the air like a windstorm. When the plane lands in this deserted city, Kashif immediately recognizes the place. It was once a city of gold, worship and excess. Now it is deserted, destroyed, bombarded, abandoned, like a forlorn planet of rock and debris.

The landing is smooth and when the door floats open, Kashif and The Messenger are escorted through a former downtown area and into an unsuspecting building. They descend further down a flight of stairs, at which point there is a glimmering elevator door, stainless steel and too modern for its rustic surroundings.

The elevator descends further towards the center of the earth until it reaches a bunker. The bunker, like the plane, is centered by a crescent table. There are men sitting at the table. One of which is recognizable to Kashif as the father of the mother of his child, the unknowing grandfather of his dying daughter. When Kashif enters the room, the entire room rises to applaud his entrance. Kashif is embarrassed by this reception. The Young Man does not applaud. He is stoic and firm in the face. He leaves the room and motions to take The Messenger with him.

"Please, he is with me."

"He will have to die, afterwards."

"I will kill him myself."

The Messenger seems like a lost child in this exchange and Kashif doesn't assure him everything will be all right. The Young Man is correct. This type of conversation, this type of knowledge is forbidden. Only a few can live to tell.

A man with albedo skin begins the proceeding. He is sitting next to his lover's father, his daughter's grandfather. His ignorance makes Kashif stronger.

"We received your blood. You are."

"Yes, I am."

"Returned."

"Yes."

"We believed you dead."

Her father is darker skinned and bearded grey. Each of the men is dressed formally. Everything appears uniform to Kashif, just as he expected. Blood will have blood. Business will have business.

"You want something," the man with white hair on the panel asks.

"Yes."

"And you will return?"

"Yes."

"What is it you want?"

"The child."

"The child is yours."

"We want something as well."

"My blood."

Kashif knew they needed his blood for much more than identification. He can feel The Messenger's curiosity behind him. Or perhaps The Messenger is reacting to the fact he will soon die. He must have persuaded himself it would never happen. The Young Man must have frightened him.

"My blood is yours."

"We will use it to complete the final stage of terror. We will recreate your genius."

His daughter's grandfather introduces this concept. Kashif refutes it nonetheless to hide his ability to read their minds.

"My blood alone will not accomplish this."

"Which is why you will join us. You will be the master teacher on this council. You will guide us into the supernatural future."

After hearing this prognostication, Kashif knows the next step is scientific in nature. Creating terror from the root up. Not just replicating it from tradition. The Nazis were well on their way to cloning an Aryan race. Other operations had already experimented with the idea. Creation. Creating terror from a cell in order to immortalize it forever, just like God created life so that it could die and rise again in a more perfect form than when it began.

The miracle child must have increased their belief in the science of the supernatural. Absolute power was only achievable on one level up until the child's discovery. Until the child arrived, they simply used faith and religion to justify violence and the assumption of power. But the arrival of the child introduced new and creative possibilities. The power to create. The fall of Lucifer. Greatness beyond The Great. The potential of their ideas and dreams.

And his blood was a link in this calculation. The evolution of his instincts needed to be a part of this new terror recipe. Supernatural terror.

"I will join you," Kashif confirms. He sees a vacated seat on the council. He assumes this seat has been reserved for him.

The council is pleased. Her father is pleased, almost proud without knowing the real reason why. Kashif wonders if The Young Man will be as pleased with his promotion to the council. Perhaps he expected it for himself. There was envy in his mannerisms. Kashif's resurrection from the dead might have interrupted his plans to achieve council status.

Kashif stands alone in the center of the bunker and he is instantly weakened by the fear that his daughter might have already perished. He doesn't know where the thought comes from. He doesn't see it coming like a bullet in the back. Perhaps this is so because he hasn't seen her for quite some time. He grows desperate to see the child and to validate his miraculous powers. His faith is weakened. His instincts are confused where it concerns her.

"Where is the child?"

The council senses his impatience. He is a desperate man before them. He doesn't resemble the man they remembered. Her unknowing grandfather is confused by this hint at weakness. Kashif wonders if they regret stealing his blood, although he didn't put up much of a fight.

The Messenger is also shocked by this sudden panic in the room. It reeks of uncertainty. He has never seen a kink in the armour of Kashif's resolve.

"He will be on the plane waiting for you. And then he will return with you."

Kashif knows he has made a mistake. He has shown weakness and a dependency on finding this miracle child for an alternative agenda. The Young Man enters the bunker. He is smirking as if having listened in on the conversation.

Kashif knows that he knows. But this weakness is necessary, just as age is necessary to introduce the greater possibility of death on the horizon.

He attempts to reclaim the mistake he made, as subtle as it was.

"Do you have his blood?"

"Yes."

"Good."

The Young Man escorts Kashif and The Messenger back to the plane. The other two are not present. A child is sitting on the seat. He is barefooted and his socks have been recently pulled off of his feet. There is a green bubble rising and shrinking from his nostril. His eyes are slanted, although not ethnically. He is disabled in a way even Kashif hadn't anticipated.

The Messenger breathes relief when he realizes they are the only ones on the plane. Kashif approaches the child and the child embraces him softly. At once, Kashif understands he has met the council's greatest enemy and the seed of its downfall.

DAY 41

"You made the miracle child like your own. Tobias."
The Man is impressed by this little trick and he understands why it is significant that the miracle child has Down syndrome.

"The extra chromosome. It makes all of the difference in the blood, in the cloning of the race. It isn't perfectly strong, which is why they value Kashif's."

I am anxious for the story to return to Bsharri, but I don't want to rush it. The funnel is getting tighter near the bottom and the speed of the water in the drain is increasing too rapidly. I have passed the deadline I first set for myself before I began the story. But that doesn't matter anymore. I understand now that my reader is far more patient with me than I ever imagined. That he or she listens in the room, often sharing the theatre with The Man. Unlike him, my reader doesn't seek a spotlight on stage, in the story. Instead, my reader appreciates the silence in the act of writing, as it is reciprocated in the pleasure of reading. On that similar ground, I have come to realize with all humility that my service, where it concerns this story, applies to you and you alone, reader.

So I decide to write the last scene tomorrow. I need a day away to revive the juice. I want to come at the ending with a vengeance, like an arsonist possessed on burning an inhabited building. As I promised in the preface, the story hasn't resolved itself and there is little hope it will. It is time to burn it down but the act doesn't feel natural now that I've built it from the ground up from my idea. And what about the rewrite? It's not like I could burn the story without giving it a chance at renovation? Is that what I'm becoming? Have I indeed grown more grey hairs as a result of writing this book, and with those hairs, a newfound wisdom?

I can honestly say I am not as angry as I was when I first started this novel. And like Kashif, I feel empowered by a new faith in my storytelling instincts.

So I have the matches in my pockets and I'm afraid I'm not ready to burn this story down to the ground just yet. I'm stalling, can you tell? I'm trying to find reason not to leave this story unresolved, or worse yet, unfinished.

An unlikely discovery, I feel like I am reading myself a story while I write it, in an out-of-body type of way. I am enjoying the act of listening as much as I am enjoying the creation of the voice.

The Messenger, Kashif and the miracle child are on their way to Bsharri. The place of the poet. And Kashif has already promised he will return to the council. He will sacrifice himself once again to save his daughter's life and serve his own creation. He will perpetuate terror, personify fear (rather literally), and be the prophet of a new age of terror. It seems like the perfect scenario for him. Save his daughter, go back to creating his living art, become reclusive within the council.

Something doesn't feel right in my gut. I am nervous about the ending. I don't know why. I can't figure it out either. Kashif will be heroic. He will save someone other than himself. He will sacrifice what he truly wants, which is to get to know his other creation, a beautiful daughter, for the sake of sustaining her life. He will contribute his blood against his own will to a cause he doesn't believe in anymore, which makes his plight tragic. And best of all, this tragic hero of mine will continue to suffer for his sins in this choice, which will justify his penance for past sins. Who knows, I may be able to reunite Kashif and his daughter in a sequel. Or have them as characters who find themselves inadvertently in another novel's world.

The possibilities are there and yet something still doesn't feel right. I feel like I am working against my own fictional instincts.

I have heard nothing about my grievance at school. The board and my union representative have put it on the back burner as a result of our contract negotiations stalling. We have been working without a contract for two years now and the Board seems more interested in not making a deal approved by the province.

My wife and I have found a balance in our expectations. We struggle some days with the frustration of teaching Tobias to walk and talk and eat real food, but we are happy our other children are affectionate to him. There is a lot of love to go around, enough to convince me I don't have to kill myself with work to forget the reality of disabilities.

I am also pleased in the classroom. I worry every day I will lose my ability to care, and as a result, lose my passion to teach, but it hasn't happened yet. I continue to entertain, amuse and educate with energy, day in and day out, and sometimes I wonder if teaching is my destiny and writing my delusion.

Furthermore, I am not as angry as I used to be. This novel has fleshed it out brilliantly and therapeutically. I suppose I can attribute some of the therapy to my sessions with The Man, but even he doesn't seem to mind not re-entering the story. I believe he understood this would happen in the end, and that he was only serviceable at the beginning in an intangible way.

It is peaceful on my walks in the dead of winter. The air is sharp and the silence is reticent. There is a belief in the air and a very serene calm to everything I do. I walk with no rush. I drive with no speed. I take my time explaining in class and I don't hurry anything anymore.

I look forward to the next day when I go to sleep and I pray when I end this novel tomorrow, this peace will not go away.

DAY 42

Despite the echo of The Man's good advice, I return to The Messenger's point of view.

He sits on the opposite end of the private jet, closer to the pilot. Kashif is sitting at the back of the plane, nearly face to face with the child. All The Messenger can hear is, "Cookie. Cookie. Not all done. Cookie."

Kashif whispers something to him and the child finds it funny, beyond hilarious. He keeps repeating himself: "Cookie, Cookie, all right. All right."

Kashif leaves him and finds a seat across from The Messenger.

"My instincts aren't aligning. I feel like we have been tricked, or will be tricked."

"Should we get him some cookies?"

Kashif does not find this funny. The Messenger reads worry on his face. Now his skin colour is changing. It resembles a shade of green with purple on the edges.

"I don't want to sound condescending, but I believe it is a matter of faith," The Messenger hints.

Kashif is listening.

"From my experience, the answer to life's paradox is faith. Tragedy will become comedy, pain will become love, death will become life, and the only common ingredient is faith that something will happen outside your understanding of it."

Kashif smirks.

"I have to kill you by my word."

"I have always had faith you would. I am ready, whenever you are."

"I am not ready."

"You want to see if he can save your daughter first. You don't want to jinx it with more blood on your hands."

"You have changed," Kashif interrupts.

"And you are starting to look the same to me," The Messenger says.

They are quiet for the remainder of the flight. The child is not. He is repeating the same words over and over again and laughing to himself.

When they reach the hospital in Bsharri, Kashif carries him up the stairs. Although the boy is only five years old, he is heavy as he straps himself to Kashif's torso with an octopus grip.

Kashif's daughter is right where they left her. She is lying in her coma, asleep. The room is clean of footprints. The Messenger glances around with the expectation of seeing Sabal, except she has disappeared for good. Even her memory is disappearing into a mythical reference or lesson.

The child is relentless.

"Cookie, cookie, cookie. All done now."

Kashif places him on his daughter's bed and the boy reaches back. He doesn't want to stay. He has a goal in mind and it appears to have chocolate chips. For some reason, The Messenger imagines the boy's favourite cookie as chocolate chip.

"What do I do?"

This is the first question Kashif has ever asked The Messenger. He is confused. He doesn't know all of the answers and by virtue of that fact, he isn't invincible to himself anymore. He is vulnerable in this moment, exposed for his humanity. He doesn't know how to communicate to this child with a mental disability, with physical disabilities, and his lack of faith overpowers his accumulated strengths. In The Messenger's eyes, his murderer will find it difficult to commit the act now. If anything, Kashif is self-afflicted, unsure, reborn you could argue, or just mortal.

The Messenger has no answers either. He tries to help Kashif force the boy to touch his daughter's nimble arm. The boy is resistant. He wants a cookie. He wants it all done, as he puts it. He introduces a new demand.

"Ride in the truck. Ride in the truck."

This request confuses Kashif some more. He didn't expect this challenge. His instincts didn't prepare him to take care of a disabled child. Everything is uncertain now. Everything is fear in the moment. The possibility of his daughter dying from her terminal disease. The possibility of not saving her. The possibility she is dying because of his sins. His faith in karma above a real creator.

"Help me," he says out loud.

It is then the boy becomes quiet. His slanted eyes become watery just as Kashif's eyes do the same. The Messenger realizes the boy with Down syndrome is sensitive to Kashif's weakness. When a tear drops from Kashif's eyes, an ocean blankets the boy's face. His nose sniffles. He reaches for Kashif's much maligned face and with his awkwardly shaped fingers, which resemble fleshy claws, he pats him on the cheek. He then reaches for Kashif to embrace him again. Kashif lifts him off the bed. He is crying into the boy's shoulders. He is squeezing him tightly, for life. The air in the room is heavy with silence but for the choppy exhale of breaths from the both of them. The Messenger can hear Kashif whispering in a singing voice to the boy.

"Here I am, Lord. It is I, Lord. I have heard you calling in the night."

As if listening in on the song as well, one her father must have heard countless times as he hid amongst his Catholic enemies, her eyes open. They are glossy and black. She sees him with the boy. She recognizes the voice above the face or she is just watching the impenetrable embrace. She doesn't signal awareness until she rises to the sitting position.

Kashif doesn't notice his daughter is awake until The Messenger forces his attention with his eyes.

The boy talks. "Cookie now. Cookie now? All right. All right."

He chuckles to himself and doesn't let Kashif see his daughter. Wherever Kashif's face moves, so does the boy's in this childish game. He wants assurance.

"Yes. Yes. Cookie, yes."

The boy releases his grip and his weight collapses to the floor. There, he claps his claw like hands in glee. He repeats the words again.

"Cookie. Cookie. Cookie. Yay!"

It is then the space is interrupted by an intruder. I don't see him coming. Neither does The Messenger, because he wouldn't be able to recognize him. He enters the room nonetheless. It is The Man. I try my best to delete what I am about to write before I write it but my fingers hold the story now outside my brain and heart's control of it.

The Man is dressed in a brand new three piece suit—black. His silver pocket watch is exposed and glimmering. In the silence of the stare, the one between Kashif and his daughter—that one, permanent, recognizable stare—The Man walks up to Kashif, pulls a gun from behind his back and puts a bullet in his head.

Kashif collapses to the floor as the child had. The sound of his weight dropping dull and dead.

The Man stares at The Messenger and The Messenger is fully aware he will be shot next. He wasn't allowed to see him in the first place. Now he can paint a description of the Man's face. His skin is pocked and his chin is sharp and the man appears to be missing a part of his tongue.

This Man is The Military Man from Kashif's childhood story. The one who stole him from his home, made him kill his own brother. The one who trained his instincts, who hardened him against the world so he could break it into pieces one day with fear and terror. This is The Military Man who has returned to destroy his creation.

The Man points the gun at The Messenger.

The Child asks for more cookies.

The Daughter believes she is in a dream.

And his last words spill out.

"I'm sorry."

Instead of firing, the Man buries the gun in his pocket, lifts the child from the floor and leaves through the door from which he came. On the child's shoes is the blood of the murderer he could have saved if there was only enough faith in the room.

Kashif's daughter finally sees The Messenger in the room. She lies her head down on the pillow and closes her eyes.

Day 43

Author's After(the End of the World)word

I search for The Man everywhere. I try to find him in my imagination, in the walk-in closet. I listen for him in the silence after I make love to my wife, but he is long gone. He invaded my story at the very end when I was most vulnerable as a writer and creator and made me true to my word in The Author's Preface.

I promised to make you feel like you lost something at the end, like you were robbed of a sentimental possession, and then he let me set fire to a story that found baptism in a flame. Some ashes remain, of course, like the surviving Messenger and the relationship between Kashif and his daughter's mother. They may rise again one day, or fade away. Or simply remind their author that he is alive and could write again.

My wife will not appreciate this part of the story and perhaps my children may question it one day in their rebellious years. As I mentioned in my Preface, I stole the story.

I was doing my M.A. in Windsor at the time when I met her. You see, when you are accepted into a Master's Program you are provided the privilege of earning some of the tuition back with a teaching position. Each of the Master's candidates is brought in to see the Dean of the Department, one on one.

In my meeting, Dr. Q, a very skinny, angular faced academic with a slow voice, presented the truth to me. As I sat before her desk, she began with small talk.

"How do you like The University of Windsor thus far?"

"I am adjusting and enjoying my courses."

"Yes. Yes."

She removed my transcript.

"Your portfolio of writing must have been impressive."

"As I'm sure were all of the others."

"No, you see, they accepted you into the program despite your overall average in your final year of undergraduate work. It is below our cut off."

"Yeah, well my father had a major accident and I spent most of my final year in the hospital watching over him in a coma."

Her smile was strained and her nod forcefully understanding while she listened. Everything in her corner office was stained wood. Oxford stained wood.

"Nonetheless, you do understand we don't have a teaching fellowship for you. We only have twelve fellowships and you are thirteen."

I wasn't stunned or even insulted at the time. I didn't even know the fellowships were paying jobs, to be honest.

"You can work part-time on the weekends in The Writing Development Center down the hall. We have some Visa students at the school, or English as Second Language students who will need help writing essays. It doesn't pay as much as the fellowship."

She revealed all of this with iceberg white teeth and a heavy, lipstick smile.

"That's fine. I'll work in the Writing Development Center."

My first student on an early Saturday morning couldn't speak English. She was dressed and jewelled, perhaps overly so for so early a session. Her hair was shiny black straightened and her eyes the match with exquisitely ornate eyelashes. Her skin was flawless and painted expertly to complete the portrait. When she walked into the closet of a room I was more than captivated. I could hear my breathing.

"Hello, and welcome."

She stared at me and raised her hand embarrassingly.

"You don't speak English?"

She nodded no.

My first student as a teacher and she knew nothing more than Hi and Bye.

I recommended she watch soap operas. This was my out-of-the-box first lesson as an English teacher. I remembered how my grandmother couldn't speak English, but she knew exactly what was happening on *The Young and the Restless*. The words matched the melodramatic expressions in soap operas. After a few weeks of this unorthodox therapy, Leia understood small talk. She learned how to write quickly and it made me believe I was a good teacher.

I slept with her before the submission of her first essay. I was in love with her. I was in love with her simplicity and her miraculous beauty.

I remember a night in particular when I chose to listen to her speak in her sleep. I marvelled that she spoke in English and not her native, Arabic tongue.

She woke up and her face had changed once she realized I was there. Drool had escaped her bottom lip to wet the pillow and she was embarrassed. I could tell she considered it unladylike, the manners instinctive within her, embedded by a higher force beyond the reprimand of a parent or an overbearing school teacher.

She stared at me with the assumption I had heard more of her confession.

"My father was a notorious terrorist. He died so I could live here."

She placed her hand on my chest and in its softness I felt my world tremble.

Acknowledgements

With so many voices functioning at the same time in this novel, I would be remise not to acknowledge all of the voices who inspired me during the process of creating this experiment. Some days I hear the voice of my grandfather, Albert, settling me down during a panic attack. My grandfather worked in a mine for $1 a day so that I could have the privilege to live and write freely in a young country. This lesson is never lost on me and it continues to motivate me to be better.

Other days, I hear my mother's wisdom through her parable-like stories, or my father's razor sharp reason from his observations on life. Thank you Leonardo and Marcella Serravalle for showing me how to stand behind my words, and for constantly reminding me where I come from. I will continue to work to the bone to honour the sacrifices made for me.

I would like to appreciate all of my students over the years whose bright-eyed faith in their teacher's dreams is just as encouraging and necessary during spouts of doubt and second-guessing. I truly hope this assortment of words justifies the belief in language I defend on a daily basis in class. On a professional level, I would like to thank supportive writers like Lauren B. Davis, Joseph Boyden, Craig Davidson, Andrew Pyper, Mark Anthony Jarman, Michelle Berry, Douglas Gibson and many others who have offered me advice, consolation, and hope over the years. Once again, I am grateful for your generosity and time.

I would like to single out Chris Needham for having the balls to publish this story. I admire your fight for art's sake, and your faith in this experimental work, and in me as a writer, makes me feel like a younger brother who gains confidence in the shadow of an older brother who believes in him.

On the brotherly note, I would be nowhere without the strongholds of Frank and Ryan Serravalle, who raise me up in esteem, but protect me from myself. Thank you for being close enough to reach whenever I am in need. I hope I have reciprocated the same over the years. And thank you for the joys of your families, Vanessa, Audrey, Sofia, Nicki, Leonardo and London. In the same familial breath my extended family, Linda (Ma), Rob, Cathryn, Gary and Margie are always there for me with concern, appreciation for my work, and care.

To my lovely wife Lauren and four kids, Aidan, Oscar, Tobias and Alaia, I can only say how sacred it is to be surrounded by the blessings of your unconditional love. I apologize for losing myself in your presence when I write, and for not expressing enough how much I appreciate the beautiful noise you create to wake me from my distractions. All of you save me from day to day.

Life comes full circle when you admit that you have become the very product of what inspired you to be in the first place. To all of the teachers who have found what I have said and written important enough to listen to and read, thank you sincerely. Ralph Serravalle, Maria Volante, Denise Rozman, Di Brandt, Mrs. Bidotchka, Mrs. Urquart, Mr. and Mrs. Prior, Mr. Hill, Dr. Reecer, Dr. Coggins, Dr. Crick, and so many more. It took me this long to realize that teaching and writing are actually the same thing—moving someone else with words of wisdom, love and passion.

Finally, I am humbled by and grateful for the whispered conversations I have with my Saviour. Let me always be an instrument for your peace and love.